A DEATH IN DURANGO

A NOVEL

DOUG TWOHILL

This book is a work of fiction. Names, characters, businesses, organizations, places, events, and incidents are either a product of the author's imagination or are used fictitiously. Any resemblance to actual persons, living or dead, events, or locales is entirely coincidental.

Published by River Grove Books
Austin, TX
www.rivergrovebooks.com

Distributed by River Grove Books

Design and composition by Greenleaf Book Group
Cover design by Greenleaf Book Group
Cover images used under license from
©istock.com/grandriver; ©Shutterstock.com/N8Allen; ©Shutterstock.com/Ihnatovich Maryia; ©Shutterstock.com/Dominic Gentilcore PhD; ©Shutterstock.com/Matyas Rehak; ©Shutterstock.com/Patrick E Planer;

Publisher's Cataloging-in-Publication data is available.

Print ISBN: 978-1-63299-558-2

eBook ISBN: 978-1-63299-559-9

First Edition

CONTENTS

ACKNOWLEDGMENTS

The English have Shakespeare, the French have Molière, the Russians have Chekhov, and we Americans have the Western.

—Robert Duvall

I would like to thank the following for inspiring this book: Larry McMurtry, Louis L'Amour, John Wayne, Woodrow Call, Gus McCrae, Waylon, Willie, Johnny, and Kris, R. J. Poteet, Charles Goodnight, James Michener, Rooster Cogburn, Shane, Meriwether Lewis, William Clark, John Colter, Butch and Sundance, Charlie Waite, Blue Bonnet Spearman, Rowdy Yates, Kit Carson, Zane Grey, Tell, Tyrel and Orrin Sackett, the Cartwrights, Marshal Dillon, Lucas McCain, the Dutton family, and many, many others too numerous to mention.

PREFACE

The tale that is told in the following pages is roughly based on the stories, facts, legends, myths, and lies of the Old West. It is by no means historically accurate or factually correct, nor intended to be so. Rather, it is intended to be accurately evocative of the pioneering *spirit* of life on the rugged frontiers of the Old West. Some people in the story are historically real, but I have no knowledge that they ever acted as depicted. Some characters are loosely based on real people, and some are made up entirely. Time lines are fungible, and places named might not exist or be where implied. Or they might have existed once long ago, but no longer do, passed over by the ages.

One thing is true. Decades ago, there was a death in Durango, and that's where this all started.

1

THE CRIME

As soon as the wheels touched the runway, the prairie dogs scattered. Dozens of them dashed about, heading for their holes and cover. Anyone who lands at La Plata airport is familiar with this unusual welcoming committee. Under normal circumstances, Jim Barlow would find them cute and humorous, but not today. He had landed at La Plata twice before. The first was the time after his daughter, Patty, had moved to Durango after college, about ten years earlier. Back then, he had helped move her belongings from New York when she decided to settle here in the Animas Valley. The second time was when he returned to help her move again, when she moved into the trailer on the ranch that she had been hired to manage for the rich sports agent from California who knew a lot about money but nothing about horses or ranching.

Those trips were different, filled with hope and possibilities for the future. His mind was spinning at the contrast as he acquired his rental SUV, pulled out on to Highway 160, and headed for the coroner's office.

Jim Barlow had done his twenty-five years as an NYPD detective and dealt with too many homicides to count. He had thought his experience gave him special insight into how the families felt when they found out a loved one was killed. That bubble burst when he got the call from the Durango sheriff that Patty had been found dead in her trailer from a self-inflicted gunshot wound.

Suicide? It made no sense. She didn't even own a gun.

Patty was his only child. She meant the world to him. When his wife left him because of what the police life does to so many marriages, Patty sided with him. Even though she lived half a continent away, they were somehow closer than ever. No matter what, he could count on her for their weekly FaceTime call. Strawberry blonde and petite, at five foot two and ninety-five pounds of adventure, Patty was always finding the edge and living on it. She had fulfilled her childhood dream of becoming an elementary school teacher. After graduating from the State University at Albany, she accepted an offer to teach in a Bronx elementary school. In the gap between graduation in May and the new school year in September, she decided to take a job as a rafting guide on the Animas River. After two weeks, she called him to say she resigned her teaching position and was going to make Durango her home.

His mind was spinning with question upon question as he pulled up to the coroner's office, nestled in an alleyway across Main Street from the train depot. Passing through the doorway, he noted the contrast to the huge coroner's office he had visited so many times in New York City. This was a small-town coroner. There was no waiting area, and as he entered, he directly stepped into the office of Dr. Preston, who was expecting him. The doctor looked and spoke a bit like the actor Wilford Brimley. Wearing a rumpled tan suit and sitting behind an antique wooden desk, he put the coffee he was drinking down so quickly he left some dripping from his overgrown mustache.

Preston had concerns about meeting with Barlow. Almost seventy, he had been coroner for more than twenty years. He had dealt with every manner of death: natural causes, ranching and farming accidents, car crashes, animal attacks, and the occasional murder. He had been around Durango long enough to know who not to cross and where not to dig too deep. Mostly, he wanted to finish out the year and retire with his wife to a little hacienda in New Mexico and collect his pension with as little trouble as possible. He feared this detective from New York was going to rock his usually calm boat.

"Mr. Barlow, I'm Bill Preston. Sorry to meet you under these circumstances and my condolences on the loss of your daughter. Everyone in the valley knew her, and never a bad word was spoken of her, so far as I ever heard, anyway. She was special."

"Thanks for your kind words, and thanks for taking the time to see me," Barlow responded politely. "I appreciate your emailing me the police report. I have been in homicide a long time. I am sure you did a great job. But you have to understand, this has been really hard for me to process. She had so many options besides taking her own life, and I never saw even a hint of that in her.

There are just a few questions I have, to tie up some loose ends. Would that be okay?"

"Sure," Preston replied, leaning forward.

"The police report says she was found in her trailer, that she had been there for several days," Barlow started. "The door was open wide enough so her body could be seen from the outside. Yet nobody missed her immediately because the ranch owner was back in LA and she was the only ranch hand on site, correct?"

Preston nodded.

"The equine veterinarian came by to treat the horses and noticed that they hadn't been fed or watered, so she went looking for Patty and found her," Barlow continued.

"That's what the report says," Preston replied.

"Well, here's the part that bothers me. Patty didn't own a gun. There was a gun recovered at the scene, but it may or may not be the same caliber as the bullet found."

Preston leaned back in his chair, not liking where this was going.

"Can I take a look at the actual weapon, bullet, and other ballistic evidence?" Barlow requested.

"Sorry," Preston replied. "The Colorado Bureau of Investigation has taken all that to Denver."

Surprised, Barlow said, "You knew I was coming. Seeing those was important to me!"

"Yes, I did. Yes, I did," Preston replied. "But here in Colorado, the CBI has final say on these things."

"Okay, let me ask you a different question," Barlow continued. "Was there anyone who might wish to harm my daughter? Anyone she was having trouble with?"

"Well." Preston paused uncomfortably, pondering what to say next. He didn't want to answer this question. But he knew that if he didn't, Barlow would find out about Buck soon enough. If he didn't answer, he would just be drawn further into the situation he was scrambling to avoid. "Don't know if Patty ever mentioned to you, but she had an on-again-off-again thing going of a sorts with Buck Strickland. I am saying this to you off the record, but folks around here couldn't figure the two of them, her being so sweet and all and Buck not having, let's say, the best reputation. Buck is a blacksmith and a farrier of sorts, shoeing the horses out there at the ranch and such. I guess it was kinda lonely out there and one thing led to another."

Patty had told him about Buck, but she didn't let on that it was anything serious.

"Where can I find this Buck? I'd like to talk to him," Barlow pressed.

Preston drew a deep breath. "I don't know for sure, but I hear he may be away. Visiting an old family friend down in Old Mexico, they tell me."

"Mexico?" Barlow said incredulously.

"Yeah," Preston answered. "The Stricklands are close with a family down there named Flores. Old man Strickland, the great-grandfather, he was in tight with old Pedro Flores. Years ago they were doing 'cattle deals' we'll just call them, way back before the railroad tracks were laid. The story is that old man Strickland saved the first Pedro Flores's life once and they've been close ever since."

"Odd that he would head out of town right after his girl was found dead," Barlow said sarcastically.

"Jim. Can I call you Jim?" Preston asked sympathetically. "Jim, I'm a dad just like you. I have a granddaughter Patty's age. I don't know what I would do if anything ever happened to her. I can see how your mind works, you being a detective and all. It must be the hardest thing in the world for a father to accept that his daughter would find life so difficult that she'd take her own life. No matter what we want to believe, we can never truly know what's going on in another person's soul, not even our own flesh and blood. You are really close to this and you're not wanting to accept what she did, God rest her soul. You might be looking for some things that just ain't there. This is a tragic suicide, Jim. That's the way I called it. That's the sheriff's ruling. That's the official finding of the state of Colorado. I hope you can find peace with that."

Barlow jumped in. "I have been trying to see the sheriff, but my calls and emails are being ignored. Any chance you can get me to see him?"

Preston stood up, signaling the meeting was ending. "The sheriff is back East at a law enforcement convention. I doubt any of the deputies will talk to you about such a sensitive case."

Deeply frustrated, Barlow nevertheless thanked Preston for his time and headed uptown on foot. He had arranged to meet Lynette Bouchard, who was Patty's best friend, at the Outlaw Bar and Grill, a gritty, Western-style saloon. As Barlow passed through the doorway, he saw a sign on the wall that read—

WELCOME TO THE OUTLAW, WHERE THE WILD WEST REMAINS

You are entering a Western establishment
We are proud of our heritage
We love our trees but don't hug 'em
We believe in God, country, and the Second Amendment
We believe the West knows what's best for the West
We do not serve lattes or vegetarian ANYTHING
If you are from California, thanks for stopping by and hope you have a safe trip home real soon
We've been getting along fine with our Native Americans and don't need any advice in that area, thank you
We have an inferiority complex; we feel city life is inferior
We think Custer was misunderstood
We'll take mountains over skyscrapers any day
And we'll pick living full over living long every time
If you can respect all that, come on in
If not, we won't miss ya
THE MANAGEMENT

A few cowboys were milling around the bar waiting for happy hour to start. Lynette Bouchard was in the gunfighter seat in the far corner with her back to the wall. Lynette was a beautiful cowgirl, a combination of Western ruggedness and natural beauty who could fit in at a rodeo or in a Ralph Lauren ad. With raven hair and hazel eyes, her skin had a touch of olive that hinted at her Native American genes, as did her high cheekbones. Lynette was second-generation Durango, but fifth generation of the West. She had befriended Patty when the two of them had competed against each other in barrel racing.

Patty had often spoken to Barlow about Lynette, and he had heard about her backstory in snippets. Lynette's ancestors had fled France for Canada during the French Revolution's Reign of Terror. A family of intellectuals, they arrived in America with few skills suitable for the New World, settling in Arcadia, Nova Scotia, where they lived a hardscrabble existence farming the rocky soil. However, it wasn't long before they were expelled by the British and forced to march 1,800 miles to New Orleans, where they tried for a fresh start in the Cajun community. As the family continued to struggle to gain an economic foothold in the gateway to the Mississippi, the oldest son, Jacques, headed west through St. Louis to try his hand at trapping for beaver and other pelts in the Rockies. Proving to be a proficient trapper, he settled in Montana and took a Blackfoot woman for his wife. Over time, some of the following generations of Bouchards drifted south, with Lynette's parents settling in the Animas Valley.

Lynette had the expression of a woman who had just lost her best friend. She greeted Barlow with a hug that brought on a sudden unexpected burst of tears to her eyes. They exchanged pleasantries and condolences, and after some small talk, Barlow got to the point.

"Tell me about Patty and Buck."

Lynette's eyes hardened. Her brain hurt as she struggled with the challenge of having to tell a story she didn't want to tell to a man who didn't want to hear what he was about to hear.

"I despise Buck Strickland," she finally started. And then the dam burst as self-control lost the battle to rage and frustration. "That man is the scum of the earth. Comes from a long line of the same. I told Patty to stay away from him. He made Patty's life hell and nobody around here wants to fess up to the fact that he might've had something to do with her death. Patty and Buck went out on and off. Patty was doing it mostly because she was lonely and there aren't a lot of desirable men out Ignacio way, near the ranch. But Buck was hotter than a black motorcycle seat in the desert for Patty and he wouldn't take no for an answer. She tried to keep him at a distance, but he wouldn't have it. Sometimes he got rough with her. She was too scared of him to go to the police. They're all friends of his anyway. When that boy drinks he gets crazy, and he is all of six foot five and two hundred eighty pounds. He finally roughed her up pretty good and she told me she'd rather be dead than live like that. So, she broke it off.

"Well, a few days later that gorgeous golden retriever, Timber, took sick, real bad sick. Not knowing what was wrong with her, Patty tried everything, but nothing worked. Finally, she carried Timber out to her truck and drove her to the vet. The vet said strychnine poisoning. Timber was too far gone to save, so they put her down. Timber died a horrible death. Took three days.

"Do you know how strychnine kills? Its god-awful. It attacks the nervous system. Shakes, seizures, then the lungs fail. It's a horrible way to die. Patty never left her side the whole time. After the poor dog was gone, Patty was walking the fence line by her trailer and found several pieces of meat laced with strychnine. That bastard Buck killed Timber just to torture her. And you know what's the worst part? The whole three days he kept calling her and texting her, saying, 'How's your dog?' Can you think of anything lower? It wasn't but two weeks later Patty was found dead—suicide they're all claiming—yet suddenly Buck is nowhere to be found."

"This stinks like hell. Why isn't anyone investigating this as a murder?" Barlow demanded.

"Because Buck is a Strickland," Lynette said with disdain.

"What does that mean?"

Lynette looked Barlow square in the eyes and offered, "I don't know what you are planning on doing about all this. If Patty was my daughter, I would want to get to the bottom of what happened to her and see that whoever is responsible pays. I knew her better than anyone in the valley. I don't know what it was, but it wasn't suicide. But before you get going, I need to give you some advice. There are two names you need to know: Vanderhorns and Stricklands. Those two families have been at it since the first white man came to this valley, and if you want to understand what happens in Durango you need to start with them. And you won't find out anything about Patty that the Stricklands don't want you to know."

2

THE VALLEY OF LOST SOULS

Barlow pulled cautiously into a visitor parking lot at Fort Meriwether College, as close as he could to the building that housed the history department. A chance encounter at breakfast at the Doubletree hotel on the river had led to an appointment with Dr. Becker, the department chairman. The professor's second-floor office was pure cowboy, decor-wise, with regional Native American memorabilia accessorizing it. His window offered a sweeping view of the valley below.

Fort Meriwether College had a unique history. Situated a thousand feet above the valley floor with a dominating view of the town and valley, it derived its name from the fact that it was built on the footprint of an old army outpost. Fort Meriwether was commissioned by President Lincoln at the outbreak of the Civil

War. Fearing an attack by the Confederates out of Texas in an attempt to seize the gold and silver of Colorado to finance the South's war effort, Lincoln sent troops to the garrison to counter any such move. The fort served as a functioning army post until the turn of the twentieth century, when it was converted to a boarding school for local Native Americans. It evolved into a trade school and agricultural academy until 1964, when it became a certified four-year college.

"Jim, I know you are wanting some closure about Patty's death," Dr. Becker began. "I don't know how much I can help on that issue, but if you are looking for the story of this valley, you've come to the right place."

Becker, who looked to be in his sixties, was a wiry man of average height, and pale for someone who spent a lot of time outdoors in the mountains and forests surrounding Durango. Behind wire-rimmed glasses, his eyes were small for his face, making his nose appear more prominent. Barlow noticed Becker was wearing top-of-the-line cowboy boots. A Stetson hung on the back of the office door.

"When I started asking about my daughter, I was told if I wanted to understand what happened I would need to know about a family called the Stricklands," Barlow said.

"Well, Jim, I must say you got to the bottom line of this town pretty quickly," Becker said. "You were told the truth. Durango and the Strickland family are inseparable. In fact, some people think the real story of our town can't be told unless you start with the Stricklands and the Vanderhorns. Those families were among the first to settle here. They have been here ever since, and have been on the opposite side of nearly everything that has happened here in the last hundred years.

"The Animas Valley," Becker went on, "where Durango is located, gets its name from the Animas River. Animas is short for the name the Spanish gave it, El Rio de las Animas Perdidas—the River of Lost Souls. It was given that name in the 1600s by a Spanish conquistador who came to this area looking for gold. The story goes that several of his men drowned in the river, and it was named for them after they died. One legend says these men were attempting to cross the river carrying a couple hundred pounds of gold from a mine they had discovered, refused to drop it when the current got too strong, and that gold was washed away with those soldiers and is still in the river somewhere waiting to be found. Some say the ghost of those dead men can be seen struggling in the river from time to time." Becker chuckled.

"The strange thing about the Animas Valley," he continued, "as beautiful as it is, for a long time it was largely ignored. It's down here in the southwest corner of Colorado, pretty as can be with a temperate climate and farmable land, yet it was one of the last places in Colorado where people settled. For two hundred years after the conquistadors passed through, it was basically ignored by white men. Interesting thing is, the Indians didn't have much use for the place either. It just kind of sat here like Eden in the Rockies, with the sun rising every day over the Sangre de Cristos and setting over the San Juans for centuries, spectacular beauty with barely a human soul to witness."

"How does that relate to the Stricklands?" Barlow said impatiently.

"I'm getting to that," Becker responded. "Let's not get ahead of ourselves. See, Colorado really didn't grow according to any kind of plan. What would happen is that gold hunters from back East, from all over the world, actually, would come out here seeking their fortune. They fanned out to the far corners of Colorado looking for claims to stake. When someone found a vein—*bam!*—overnight a town started as fortune hunters from everywhere rushed in to try their luck. That's where the phrase 'gold rush' comes from."

"So, the Stricklands were gold miners?"

"No, not at all. See the thing is, when you look at all the gold rushes that ever happened, more money was spent trying to find the gold than was ever taken out of the ground. You know who was the richest man to come out of the California gold rush of '49? Levi Strauss. Never set foot in a mine, but he made money off of every one of those miners, selling them picks and shovels and tents and the jeans that they sell even to this day. When a town goes from two hundred to twenty thousand overnight, those miners need to be outfitted and supplied and entertained and such. You can't grow food at altitudes like Silverton and Ouray and the like. Or so people thought at the time.

"Then one day Zane Vanderhorn came to the valley, an escort to a shipment of supplies from Denver by wagon, where it would be broken out onto mules to take up to the mining camps. His family was in farming and dry goods back in Ohio, and when he saw the valley and the river, well, he fell in love with the place. It has been said that the first time he saw a sunset reflect on the red cliffs he told everyone he wanted to be buried right there at the base of those cliffs.

"More important, though, when he saw the four little storefronts in the town, well, he knew an economic opportunity when he saw one and staked his claim. Only his claim wasn't gold; it was commerce. Pretty soon he had a general store and a stable up and running. That was the beginning of Vanderhorn Enterprises, which is a big deal in Colorado today. Zane set up a couple of farmers on credit to show it could be done successfully in these parts. The farms worked out all right and so more farmers came and there was food aplenty. It wasn't long before both the locals and the miners were beating a path to his door."

"When did the Stricklands come in?" Barlow pressed.

Becker pulled all the pieces together. "Here's the way it works in the West. As soon as you get more than four cowboys living somewhere, somebody decides they need a saloon and a whorehouse. Bart Strickland, he came from back East to meet that need. No one knows for sure where he came from, but lots of rumors flew around that he was on the run and had changed his name. What *was* for sure was that he was a brute of a man, all of six foot four and two hundred eighty pounds, with a big scar down his left cheek and a huge handlebar mustache. He had a stare that could burn through steel, and people crossed the street when they saw him coming. He was mean as a snake, had no friends at all, and didn't care a lick what people thought.

"From the beginning, the Vanderhorns had more or less set about caring for the basic needs in the valley, while the Stricklands, you might say, took care of the baser needs of the community." Becker chuckled again, a habit that was beginning to irritate Barlow.

"Durango was soon the entertainment and social center, as well as the breadbasket for all the mining camps for miles around. And miners aren't vegetarians, you see. What they wanted was beef. So, the next smart move was for a man with vision to bring in cattle. And that's where the trouble between the Vanderhorns and Stricklands really started."

"So, it was over cattle?" Barlow asked.

Easing back in his chair, Becker grinned. "Only indirectly," he said provocatively. "It was actually over a girl."

3

RANGE WARS

Throughout history, wars have been fought for a number of reasons: conquest, resources, food, slaves, territorialism, to name a few. A few times in history, men found a woman desirable enough to go to war over. Most notably, the entire country of Greece and the city of Troy fought a war because two men lusted over the same Helen.

There was a war fought over such a woman in Durango. Her name was Charlotte McClintock.

Charlotte was seventeen when she arrived in Durango, brought into civilization, such as it was at the time, by some Good Samaritans. They had found her wandering, hungry and disheveled, alone in the wilderness, carrying her only possessions in a makeshift sack. Her parents, after two years of homesteading, had died of some unknown, virulent illness. Her younger brother,

Sean, had headed north from their small farm near Ridgway to get supplies and never returned.

Like most girls her age with no one to look after and provide for them, she had dim prospects and little hope for the future. But Charlotte had one thing going for her: charm. Most girls and women in the West of the 1800s lived a hard life, and the pain and suffering they knew showed in their attitude and on their faces. But Charlotte was different. Though she, too, had known hardship and suffering, she retained a unique appeal and zest for life that was apparent to all who encountered her. It would be fair to say she was only slightly above average in beauty. But her appearance was enhanced by a quick smile, subtle dimples in her slightly freckled cheeks, and blazing red hair. This was all the more appealing due to her habit of swaying slightly as she spoke, slowly, rhythmically shifting her weight from hip to hip, almost imperceptibly, in a manner that wasn't quite a dance but wasn't actually not, either.

Zane Vanderhorn spotted her as soon as she stepped down from the wagon in front of his store. Since there were seven men for every woman in Colorado at the time, and a good number of those were whores he was not in the habit of visiting, he didn't have much experience with women or romance, so the feelings that surged in him were new and strange. His mind couldn't find the words for this complex mix of magnetic attraction and lust and romance. The best he could do to capture the feeling was mutter to himself, "I'm gonna marry that girl."

But beneath her obvious charm, Charlotte was a levelheaded and practical girl. Though she had become the focus of attention of every single man in the area, she quickly read the signs and concluded that Zane Vanderhorn had sound prospects that distinguished him as a good one to hitch her wagon to. He was of solid character and reputation, practiced notable personal hygiene, and was the owner of several thriving businesses. It didn't hurt at all that he was tall and handsome and kind, if somewhat short on words or sophistication. She was able to get a job doing laundry and helping serve food at what was beginning to be the makings of a hotel across the street from Zane's storefront. They would see each other now and then during the days; Charlotte made sure of it. Zane properly courted her at nights. Everyone in town came to understand that Zane and Charlotte were an item, and that marriage was likely in their future.

Everyone, that is, but Bart Strickland. Bart wanted Charlotte too. But not the way Zane wanted her. Bart wanted her in the way he had used many other women—not driven by romance or love but by a mix of lust and violence. More than once, he had taken a woman who didn't want to be taken, and that circumstance made the conquest all the more satisfying to him. Charlotte was good and innocent and pure. He hated that about her and wanted to take it all from her in the worst way.

Right now, Zane Vanderhorn stood in his way. Men who had stood in his way before hadn't fared well. But Vanderhorn was an unknown entity as far as fighting and shooting were concerned, and even Bart understood that getting into a skirmish with one of the most important and respected men in the town would likely be to his own detriment. So he thought it best to bide his time and wait for a chance to ambush Zane on a trail or push him down a well if the opportunity presented itself.

An opportunity to win over Charlotte's heart was about to arrive in an unforeseen way, even though it wasn't her heart Bart was after.

Cattle ranching was becoming a big business along the Colorado–New Mexico border. Loosely defined ranches with overlapping claims to land—and sometimes to the cattle themselves—were commonplace. Now and then, tensions would arise between various factions of cowboys over who owned what. Tension was running particularly high between Durango's cattlemen and the ranchers in nearby Farmington, over in New Mexico. It came to a boil when a few cowboys got roughed up and some shots were fired out on the range.

Drew Jenkins, a leader of the Farmington cattlemen, felt that steps needed to be taken to deescalate the situation. He decided to bring a delegation of representatives to Durango, meet with their counterparts, and come to an understanding of how to ranch harmoniously and avoid conflict. Knowing that twelve armed men on horseback approaching a town unannounced might be misconstrued, they sent an emissary in advance to let Durango know their intentions.

Unfortunately, when their messenger arrived in Durango, the person he informed was Bart Strickland, owner of the Broken Mustang saloon. As soon as he had fulfilled his task to deliver the message, he went to the saloon and got drunk.

A plan quickly formed in Bart's devious mind.

"Raiders coming!" he yelled to all who would hear. "To arms! To arms!"

As sincerely as he could fake it, he informed Durango that an army was at that very moment on its way from Farmington to wreak vengeance on their town. Quickly, he recruited a group of about a dozen men, mostly from among those drinking in his saloon, with a promise of free drinks when they got back, and they headed out of town to meet the invaders.

Thus began the Battle of the South Mesa.

Bart and his band of mostly drunken recruits, having the advantage of surprise, determined to sit in ambush and make quick work of the New Mexican "invaders," and then return to town as celebrated heroes. Bart picked a spot where the trail ran close to a small rock ledge rising about six feet above the trail, which would be perfect for concealment. All they needed to do was get into position and wait for the right moment to kill their unsuspecting visitors in a hailstorm of lead.

Jenkins and the Farmington men approached, two by two. They were riding casually, since they were on a peace-offering mission with not a thought in the world that a gun battle was about to begin. They were within twenty yards, with Bart about to ignite the ambush, when suddenly one of his recruits, Shorty Higgins, probably due to his heavy drinking earlier, lost track of their mission and stood up to take a piss. As he dropped his trousers to do his business, he looked up to see the shocked New Mexicans before him. Partly remembering through a drunken fog why he was there, he reached down with both hands, struggling to retrieve his Colt 45 from his dropped gun belt, frantically yelling, "Ambush! Ambush!"

The Farmington men, thanks to Shorty's warning, dove for cover. And the battle, such as it was, was on. On one side were the Durango men, mostly drunk stragglers who had little allegiance to

Durango or Strickland and had rarely shot their pistols in anger. On the other were the Farmington men, who didn't know who their adversary was or why they were being shot at, or why the man with no pants had warned them. For two and a half hours, the two sides exchanged fire. Due to lack of fighting ability and motive and killer instinct, the combatants gradually lost interest in the fight. One man on each side was slightly wounded, but no one was killed. As water and bullets became scarce under the blazing hot sun, a white flag was raised. Jenkins and Strickland parleyed and agreed to call the battle a draw, and that both sides would agree to all the terms Farmington had come to deliver. Both "armies" left the field. Bart Strickland and his band of drunks returned to Durango, where they held a huge celebration of their tremendous victory. Each participant got to tell their story of bravery and courage under fire and how they saved the town. With each telling, the body count of New Mexican dead grew. And there was no bigger hero than their leader, Bart Strickland, who had started the whole fake battle just to win a girl.

And his plan was working. Bart Strickland, suspected rustler and outlaw of dubious past and reputation, even questionable identity, was suddenly the center of attention in Durango. All eyes were on him, including the eyes of Charlotte McClintock. In the excitement of the moment, Zane Vanderhorn was completely forgotten. Charlotte had never known a bona fide *hero* before, and when Strickland asked her to be his guest at the celebration dinner, she eagerly agreed.

The party was held at the Broken Mustang saloon. The whole town was invited to eat, drink, and dance, to celebrate the great victory over Farmington. Nearly a hundred of the townsfolk crammed into the main room to honor their brave fighting men, especially their newly minted leader. After much partying, feasting, speech-giving, and congratulating, Bart told Charlotte he had a special gift for her in his office.

Naively, she went along. They were barely through the door when he was on her, pawing at her bottom and clothes as he kicked the door closed behind them. She tried to scream, but he clasped his huge hand across her mouth. As he fumbled with his belt and her undergarments, he pushed her facedown on the desk. He pressed his cheek against hers and the smell of whiskey and tobacco and rotten teeth almost caused her to vomit. Strickland was more than double her body weight, and all her efforts to fight him off were in vain. Her heart broke as she could feel herself losing to him, powerless to stop him from taking away something she could never have again. And then he stopped.

Charlotte, in disbelief, opened her eyes and turned. There stood Bart with his pants down, dumbfounded, both of his meaty hands held pathetically over the top of his head. Behind him stood Zane with the barrel of his Colt pressed against Strickland's temple.

"We'll be leaving now," Zane said to both Charlotte and Bart. "And we will never speak of this again."

By his intervention, Zane had accomplished two things. He had saved the virtue of the woman he loved by rescuing her from a foolish girlhood infatuation. They would be married the following Sunday.

And, in Bart Strickland, he made a sworn enemy for life.

No longer being able to have Charlotte became an obsession for Bart. Although it didn't seem possible, he became even meaner, more ornery, and downright spiteful. He took up with one of his whores, named Slow Eyed Mary.

She was called Slow Eyed Mary because, not surprisingly, she had a slow eye. Her eyes didn't move in unison. Her left eye moved normally, but her right eye, plagued by some sort of muscular deficiency, couldn't keep up. Born with this imperfection, she was destined to be a prostitute. That might seem like a curse to most women, but to her it was a blessing in a way. Most women who wound up working as prostitutes in the West were desperate, penniless girls who, due to some curse of fate, simply fell into the profession. Not Mary. From her earliest days she knew she wouldn't amount to anything more than a whore, and she accepted her destiny. There was no fall from grace. There was just a natural path. And, since prostitution was going to be her livelihood, she jumped in with gusto and did her best to be the best ride money could buy. The cowboys liked her enthusiasm. And there was one thing about a poke with Mary that stood out: her slow eye. Specifically, when the action heated up, her slow eye would start rotating wildly, turning in big circles in her eye socket. When the action peaked, that eyeball would bounce around in its socket like a bullet ricocheting around in a cave.

Bart liked the thing that her eyeball did when he went for a ride, so he put her up in a small cabin of her own behind the saloon. Not that he was ever loyal to her, but they were together enough for her to bear him three sons, to whom she bestowed the biblical names of Caleb, Joshua, and Jake—somewhat ironically, given that she was a whore who never been to a church in her life. Bart never cared enough for her to give her his name, but in a way that was uncharacteristically admirable, he called the boys his own. All the years they were together, Bart relentlessly reminded Slow Eyed Mary that the only reason they were together was because he couldn't have Charlotte McClintock, who was all the woman Mary could never be. And so Mary came to hate Charlotte Vanderhorn with all her being. She raised her three boys to hate everything Vanderhorn. That hate would shape the future of the valley for generations to come.

4

THE CLIFF PEOPLE (400 A.D.)

Matu was desperate. Overheated in the unforgiving sun, he had pushed himself to near exhaustion on the long climb from the desert floor to the mesa. Every fiber in his body screamed for him to stop, but stopping could mean death for him and his people. The lowlands that had been their home since the beginning had suddenly become too dangerous, and they needed a new place to live where they would be safe from their newfound enemies.

Our People, as they called themselves, had scratched out a subsistence living in the lowlands near the creek. For a generation, several hundred of them had lived in relative peace and simplicity. But their calm, desperate lives were shattered two moons earlier when the Big Ones from the north found them. Matu was barely five foot five, but in his tribe he was among the tallest and strongest. The Big Ones, at least the ones who raided their villages and farm fields, were all nearly six feet tall and enormous in strength and fighting ability and savagery. What followed were endless attacks on Our People, in which their food, animals, and women were taken, and their men were slaughtered and mutilated to spread terror and intimidation. Our People were agrarians, not warriors. They didn't stand a chance.

Alo, the shaman, had a vision that Our People's future was up on the mesa.

"Follow Eagle to the land above," Alo had said. "Eagle will lead you to a new home for Our People."

The idea was stunning, as none of Our People had ever ventured onto the unknown mesa. Their brief oral history was filled with stories of dangerous spirits and creatures and foreboding in that place. Matu knew full well the risks and the stories and the danger of this journey. Yet any reluctance was overshadowed by the honor of being selected to scout their future, as well as the knowledge that, without a new place to live, Our People would be wiped from the face of the earth by this new enemy.

After a night sleeping under the stars, and with his food and water supplies dwindling, Matu worked his way deeper and deeper across the mesa. A great distance in, he came across a rift in the plateau, a sheer drop of a thousand feet or more. Below he could see some sparse trees and vegetation. Water!

Understanding the implications for Our People, he searched to find a way down. When he found a crack in the face of the cliff, just large enough to accommodate a man, he shimmied down the shoot and into the valley below. When he reached level ground, he looked around in awe. To his right was the sheer cliff face back up to the mesa top. Beneath his feet was a level surface about a hundred feet wide. To the left was a drop-off of several hundred more feet to the valley floor.

Matu thought long and hard. Could this be the place that Alo had seen in his vision? Matu considered this for a long time. Suddenly, an eagle appeared from the west, floated through the valley air, and landed in a nest built where the overhang of the rim formed a natural protective roof.

Matu slowly climbed the cliff face to approach the nest. As he got closer, he noticed that the rocks were moist, then wet. A few feet higher, he found a small pool of water. There was a seep from the mesa above, forming the pool. With a little luck, he thought, this seep and ones like it, along with the water in the valley below, could be enough to sustain Our People! The overhang from the plateau above would provide a natural ceiling and protect them from the elements, and enemies, if necessary. This valley was so remote, no enemy would care to look for them. Down below, in the valley itself, stretched acres of fertile ground for farming, enough to sustain their tribe. Alo had a strong vision. Yes, this could be their new home.

Matu's heart raced. He couldn't wait to tell Our People and bring them to safety. Before he climbed out of the bottom of the shoot, he took a sharp rock and scratched in the cliff face the symbol of Our People. This would be the sign to his people that they had found their new home. Back at the top of the crevice in the cliff, he carefully noted the unique geographical features so he could direct the tribe to this spot. He noticed a high spot in the mesa with three boulders and two small twisted trees; this would be his landmark.

Matu returned to his people with the great tale that the shaman's vision was true. And so, on the given day, Our People began dismantling their village in the lowlands, in preparation for leaving the next morning at sunrise, when they would carry everything out along the dangerous trail to the mesa, three days' travel away. As they proceeded, they were careful to cover their tracks so as not to be followed by the Big Ones.

Matu had given them precise directions, but he himself was not able to return with them. In one of the saddest and most ironic tragedies ever to befall Our People, Matu was killed in a brief but fatal raid by the Big Ones the very night before the journey began. His final courageous act had been to protect his wife, Fara, from the rape and the wrath of the raiders.

Three months pregnant and mourning for her murdered husband, Fara bravely made the long, hard trek up the mesa and to the cliffs that Matu had promised would be their new home. His directions and landmarks proved true. Our People built a thriving community under the cliffs. In time, they succeeded not only in farming the rich valley below, but also managed to successfully cultivate certain areas atop the mesa. They built ladders up to the mesa top and down to the valley floor that could be withdrawn to deny access to any enemy that approached, from either direction, yet none ever came. Our People thrived in their new home. The tribe grew manyfold, until more than eight thousand people inhabited the cliffs, thriving in this valley and in other valleys in the surrounding area. Matu's name, and his ultimate sacrifice for his people, was remembered around the evening fires, and he was celebrated for being the one who braved the unknown and found this sanctuary. His son—the one whom Fara had carried on the arduous journey into the mesa—later became chief of the tribe. His name was Calain, a name that means warrior, but he was always referred to as the son of the great Matu.

Under Calain's leadership, Our People set about to make a permanent settlement. In doing so, they built what would become a World Heritage site. Using the cliff overhang as a ceiling and adobe bricks for walls, they built what would ultimately be called Cliff Palace and Spruce Tree House, and dozens of other dwellings that would one day become Mesa Verde National Park.

Our People lived and thrived in this place that Alo saw in his vision, and Matu bravely discovered, and Calain built into a real and true home. Our People called the mesa home for over seven hundred years.

And then, they disappeared.

5

CATTLE DEALS

The Battle of the South Mesa, such as it was, did little to interfere with the cattle business in the valley and the plains beyond. The dustup between Durango and New Mexico was small potatoes, a few cattle changing hands under questionable circumstances, the sort of thing that was mostly accepted as a cost of doing business. Besides, what few cattle there were in the area at that time, compared to a place like Texas, really wasn't worth getting too worked up about, and certainly not worth getting killed over.

But change was coming.

Down in Fort Belknap, Texas, two enterprising cattlemen had a vision to drive herds of cattle from Texas up through New Mexico and Colorado and into Wyoming and Montana. Cattle were scarce in those parts, and they would find a profitable market for their Texas longhorns, both for food and for seeding new ranches to the north.

Charles Goodnight and Oliver Loving had an audacious plan. First, with the help of eighteen cowboys, they would drive two thousand head of cattle north across the Llano Estacado. In English, that is the "staked plains"—a region so dry and flat and desolate that stakes had been driven into the ground as route markers. Without those markers, travelers would lose their bearings and walk in circles until they collapsed and died. Encompassing 37,000 square miles of West Texas and New Mexico, the Llano Estacado is a bone-dry, alkaline-filled dust bowl of unforgiving wasteland. For over eighty miles there was not a drop of water. The only reason Goodnight and Loving were crazy enough to pick that route was because of the safety it offered from attacks and raids. Neither bandits nor Comanches would venture across that plain unless it was absolutely necessary. Next, Goodnight and Loving would enter the Comancheria, where roaming bands of warriors presented mortal danger. Further on into Colorado, the trail crossed outlaw territory, where raids and ambushes were both common and likely.

Charles Goodnight was born back East and moved to Texas when he was ten. He grew up on horses and ranches and mastered all the cowboy skills, including cigar smoking, often consuming thirty in a day. At twenty, he joined Colonel McNealy and the Texas Rangers. His first claim to fame was leading the raid that rescued Cynthia Ann Parker from twenty years of captivity with the Comanche. During the Civil War, he served on the side of the Confederacy. No fan of slavery, he never left the state of Texas or saw combat during the war. Eager to stabilize his finances in the terrible economy of the losing states after the war, he dreamed up the idea to transport Texas cattle to new markets that others thought were too risky to try.

It was on the first drive that Charles Goodnight made his mark on culinary history. Knowing that cowboys on a drive need to be well fed, and food could be scarce, he dedicated a wagon and a hired cook to the feeding of his cowboys. Named after its inventor, the "chuck wagon" became a fixture on cattle drives from then on. When being recruited for a drive, cowboys were known to ask who the cook was before asking what the pay was. The chuck wagon served two purposes. It was used to keep the cowboys well fed, of course. But it also acted as a compass. Every night before lights out, the cook's last job was to point the tongue of the horse harness toward the North Star to act as a guide star compass for the next day.

Oliver Loving was decades older than Goodnight. He had a relatively prosperous ranch and when the war broke out, he became a major supplier of beef to the Confederacy. When General Lee surrendered to end the war, Loving was left with over $125,000 in debts with no way to pay. In desperate straits, he remembered Goodnight as a young cowhand who had worked well with him before the war. Together they devised the audacious plan that would make them legends and create a trail that bore their name.

The first drive, in 1866, was wild in its ambition. Goodnight and Loving might as well have been Lewis and Clark, or Christopher

Columbus, for the daring of it all. They were able to deliver their cattle first to Fort Sumner in New Mexico, where the army desperately needed food to feed the Navajo who had been forced on to a reservation, where they had neither the expertise nor the resources to farm the land. Unable to secure an acceptable price for all the beef, Goodnight continued on to Colorado, where he sold the rest of the herd for a fat profit. Goodnight would return to Texas after that first drive with $12,000 in gold and the vision to build his next herd.

Oliver Loving and his partner, "One-Arm" Bill Wilson, headed back to Texas while Goodnight headed north. On their way back they were ambushed by a Comanche war party. A three-day battle of fight and run ensued. They eventually eluded the warriors, but Loving had serious wounds in his leg that became infected. One-Arm Bill got him to a doctor, but the infection had spread. Loving refused amputation and died at Fort Sumner, where he was buried by the army in the graveyard near the fort. When Goodnight stopped at the fort on his return trip several months later and learned of Loving's fate, he had the body dug up and personally accompanied it to Greenwood Cemetery in Texas, the place Loving had called home.

"Texans get buried in Texas," Goodnight stated adamantly.

Legend has it that when Goodnight buried Loving, he placed a sack in the grave that contained six thousand dollars in gold as a half share in the reward of having blazed the trail north. The story traveled throughout the West, and eventually grave robbers dug up the body and broke into the casket. Only they know whether or not the gold was really there.

The trail that Goodnight and Loving blazed passed east of Durango. In a stretch that had been barely traveled before, now there were thousands of heads of cattle passing through every year. While not particularly close to Durango, the now bustling trail was nevertheless close enough that Bart Strickland sensed an opportunity.

"Boys, so far we've been playing small potatoes," Strickland told his gang. "Rustling a cow here and a steer there from the locals. All those cattle on the trail all the time gives us a big opportunity. Around here, when we take even a few head here and there, it gets noticed. With all those passing through, we could set ourselves up for a real score.

"If we grab a few head at a time off the trail out there in the east, we can drive 'em back west over Wolf Creek Pass and set up a place to hold 'em. Once we get a goodly number, we'll move 'em on out and sell 'em as our own."

The biggest obstacle they faced was to find a place where it would be easy to sell stolen cattle without a lot of questions being asked. Strickland couldn't sell in any of the markets frequented by the Texas ranchers, as he would be caught easily and hanged. The place to sell was the missing piece to the puzzle, and that piece was about to fall into place.

Pedro Flores was a man with a plan. He had a vision to start a cattle ranch in Old Mexico. The problem was, no one in Texas would help him get started, fearing any manner of competition. In consultation with his family, he decided to learn the cattle business from the inside. He traveled north with Goodnight and a large herd, serving as a vaquero and scout. He kept a keen eye on every detail. On his way home, he detoured to Durango, where he met Bart Strickland, and from that meeting sprang two crime dynasties.

When Pedro Flores entered the Broken Mustang saloon, attention was paid. Most Mexicans in Durango stayed out of the white part of town unless absolutely necessary. Not that there was any particular animosity toward Mexicans in the town; it's just the way it was. Mexicans, along with a few blacks who had journeyed West to enjoy new freedoms after the war and a small number of Chinese who ran laundry and food services, and opium dens, tended to congregate together below Third Street, which was known locally as "South of the Border." There were some scuffles between the races, but it typically wasn't racial, no different than when the cowhands from two different ranches squared off.

Flores stepped to the bar and ordered a beer.

"Hey, Greaser! What you doing in my town, drinking in a white man's saloon?" came the voice of some no-name cowboy sitting at a table, drinking and carousing with a few others who rode for the Lazy T.

"I'm talking to you!" came the voice again.

Sizing up the situation, Pedro considered his options and chose calm.

"I am just finished bringing cattle up from Texas with Charles Goodnight," Pedro responded with a confident smile. "I am just making my way back to Texas, thought I'd have a drink."

"That drink is on me," said a different voice, as a large, imposing figure with a scar on his left cheek approached Pedro, his hand extended.

Long into the night, Strickland and Flores discussed the Goodnight operation in detail. By now, other Texans were also driving herds north, all more or less following his blueprint. As the details were shared and discussed, a plan came to mind. Theirs would be a plan of stealth. No big raids. Just hit all the herds coming by, a few head here and a few head there, in numbers that no one would really miss. Combined with the usual number of "strays" taken from the Durango ranchers, a large herd over time could be assembled. That herd would be taken even farther west on the Llano Estacado through New Mexico, bypassing Texas entirely, and then straight on to Juarez, where the Flores family ranch was waiting.

The plan was cunning. No one would look for the stolen cattle back where they had come from in the south. Mexicans didn't care much about brands, and paid them no heed. With a little luck and patience, Strickland and Flores would be rich. It was dangerous work, but the payoff would be worth the risk. So began the rustling, or "cattle deals," as the two crime bosses called it. A dozen cattle in one raid, a half dozen the next; never too greedy, always discreet.

On one of the drives to Mexico, Something Smith, a curious drifter who had fought for the Confederacy, was riding point. No one knew his real name, but he came to be called "Something" because his knee-jerk response to any news or facts presented to him whatsoever always got the same reply: "Ain't that something?"

As the drive wound down for the day, Something rode up to Bart Strickland and exclaimed loudly, "Since we're doing the opposite of old Charles Goodnight on the Goodnight Trail, we should call 'arn the Good Morning Trail! Ain't that something?" He let out a huge and out-of-proportion open-mouthed guffaw that revealed all of Something's missing teeth. And among outlaws and rustlers, the name stuck.

The two crime families had a very lucrative deal going. Slowly they were getting rich. But as so often happens in moneymaking schemes, the money looked so easy that impatience kicked in. Against Flores's advice, the gang got greedy, taking bigger and bigger chances and cutting larger numbers from the passing herds. Soon enough, the Texas ranchers could not ignore the rustling any longer. Charles Goodnight couldn't tolerate that common criminals and thieves were abusing the trail he had blazed. When word got back to him about the Good Morning Trail name, his temper flared like a hot branding iron. Goodnight was well known and highly respected throughout the region, and his reputation mattered to him enormously. After Loving's death, he had entered into a new partnership with John Chisum of New Mexico. Nor would it serve him well, by any means, to be seen as weak.

"Enough is enough," he said, a man of few words, yet a man who meant every single word he ever spoke.

The next drive north proceeded like all the others as it passed east of Durango. Strickland, Flores, and their men gathered along a dry, sunken arroyo, to the west and just out of sight of the dusty trail, waiting to pick off stragglers as they wandered. As was becoming his custom, Strickland pushed perilously closer to the herd, hoping to increase his yield. As they led their stolen cattle away from the main herd, a volley of shots rang out.

"Ambush!" someone yelled, anguish and fear evident in his voice.

Out of pride and spite, Goodnight had hired a group of retired Texas Rangers to put an end to rustling on the trail that bore his name. First one, then two, then three of the rustlers fell from their saddles, shot dead as the Rangers' bullets found their marks. The others scattered chaotically in every direction, while Strickland and Flores managed to stick together as they galloped, hell-bent for leather, toward the south.

The two rode at a furious pace until they reached Wolf Creek, where they made a frantic effort to ford. But before they got halfway across, a Ranger's Winchester found its mark, the force of impact flinging Pedro Flores off his horse and into the stream with a bullet lodged deep in his left thigh. Bart Strickland turned to see the current rapidly taking his partner downstream. What he did next was not of decency or of courage, but of pure greed. Knowing that without Pedro he could not continue his operation, he turned his horse around amid a hail of gunfire, and with his powerful right arm he scooped Pedro out of the river. Then, flinging the wounded man onto the back of his saddle, Strickland wheeled his horse around on its two hind legs and hightailed it across the creek and off into the dusk, saving Flores's life and cementing the partnership between these two families that would continue for almost a hundred years.

In his swagger and his arrogance, Bart Strickland would never say in public whether or not the Ranger ambush that had cost him the lives of three of his gang, and nearly that of his partner, was his last foray into cattle rustling. The Goodnight-Loving cattle trail was, after all, over two thousand miles long, and it was impractical, in reality impossible, for Charles Goodnight to position guards along its entire length. Nor was it the only vulnerable trail used for moving longhorns.

Privately, however, Strickland and Flores acknowledged that rustling had become too dangerous to continue, especially since there were so many other less hazardous ways to make a buck. Fortunately for them, although not so much for the law-abiding citizens of the region, the two partners had amassed enough money and influence to underwrite a wide variety of scams and schemes that would take their criminal enterprises to new heights. Masterminded by Strickland, their "mischief" would become a blight on southwest Colorado in the decades to come.

As for Pedro Flores, he might have gone back to Old Mexico for good, but something kept him in Durango. Her name was Lupita Chavez. Grudgingly allowed, but not really welcomed in the white saloons and other, more respectable establishments north of the border, Flores obligingly gravitated to the Mexican part of town, and that was where he met Lupita. Theirs was an immediate attraction, and their love was like a prairie fire. She was young and stunningly beautiful. He was the bravest and most dashing man she had ever met. Pedro Flores always had money to spend, and spend on her he did. More often than not, there were long periods when Pedro was away. But when Pedro and Lupita were together, they were like a volcano, heated, volatile, boiling over for each other. The memories of the days they were able to be together were enough to keep her romance embers burning during the long, lonely months they were apart, until he would return.

But then he didn't.

One day he left, giving her a long, passionate kiss and a promise to see her soon. But that return never happened. Though she would live for decades more, part of Lupita's heart died when her vaquero headed south that last time. No one would ever again light her heart ablaze like he did. She never let anyone try. Her love for him was a consuming fire, and when it passed, it left no tinder where the love for another could be sparked. Most nights, she passed the sunsets with her eyes cast to the long gray ridge that ran along the southern horizon, waiting and hoping against hope to see her Pedro returning to cure the aching in her heart. As is often true with women, she thought about her lover every day for the rest of her life.

And, as is often true with men, Pedro never thought of her again.

Nine months after he left, Lupita gave birth to a baby girl. She named her daughter Amorosa. In future years, people who visited Durango would talk about the beauty of this valley of lost souls: the red cliffs reflecting at sunset, the aspens shaking as summer turned to fall, the majestic snow-covered peaks. But all agreed there was no more beautiful sight in all of Colorado than the face of Amorosa Chavez.

6

THE GREEK

It was early spring, after Zane and Charlotte married, when a bedraggled traveler approached the Vanderhorn stable. The man dragged himself up to the barn door on bare, bloody feet, with only the clothes on his back and his mule, which he led by a short length of rope, with no saddle or saddlebags.

"Can you spare a meal for a man and animal who have fallen on hard times?" he asked in a sorrowful voice, his hand quivering as he reached out for the help he hoped to receive.

If ever there was someone in need of help, it was surely this man, Zane thought. He led the stranger inside the house, where he fetched him a hot cup of coffee and some biscuits. The man ate each biscuit in one gulp, so quickly that Zane was afraid he would choke. After Zane set up the man's mule with water and oats, he returned to his visitor.

"Looks like you've been through it," Zane said compassionately, trying to coax a little friendly conversation out of the haggard man.

"Zane Vanderhorn," he said, extending his right hand, before he delivered another round of coffee and grub.

"I'll say," responded the stranger. "My name is Constantine—you know, like the emperor—but everyone just calls me the Greek. Never expected anything like this. I thank you kindly. Thought I was gonna die for sure."

"What happened?" Zane inquired.

The Greek took a deep breath. "I was camping out by the Vallecito Lake, just passing through, really. I had just set up for the night. Nice little spot next to the lake. I made a little fire, under a fir tree to filter the smoke so no one would see it. I was fryin' me some bacon and I guess they caught scent and found me."

"Who found you?" Zane asked, as the Greek gulped down another biscuit.

The Greek's face filled with rage. "Four of the meanest sons of bitches ever to walk the earth. Two white men and two renegades. Not a half a heart among the four of them. They came into my camp and first thing, they took to whoopin' on me, all four at once." He started to cry. "There was no need for that. They coulda had anything they wanted; I couldn't have stopped them. I heard them talking they were gonna stake me out and burn me. God, I was scared. They started going through my stuff and taking all my things; they robbed me blind. I thought I was a goner for sure."

"What did you do?" Zane asked in astonishment.

The Greek shuddered, composed himself, and said, "I couldn't do nothing. I watched them whittlin' the stakes and fueling the fire to do me in, when one of the renegades going through my saddlebag chanced upon my statue of St. Christopher."

"The patron saint of travelers," Zane remarked.

"That's right, sir," the Greek continued. "Anyway, it spooked him real bad. He started ranting and fussing, said it was big medicine and if they harmed me, they would be cursed. So, they decided to rob me of everything but my shirt and pants and mule, and set me off into the wild with the warning that if they saw me again they would kill me for sure. I've been four days on foot to get here."

"Lucky break for you," Zane offered.

The Greek got really quiet, paused, took a deep breath, and promptly swallowed his fifth biscuit. "Lucky for me, not so lucky for that poor boy they had with them." His eyes filled with tears.

"What boy?" Zane demanded, lurching forward.

Taken aback by his benefactor's sudden burst of anger, the Greek could barely speak. "They had a boy with them," he stammered. "Kept the poor kid on a leash. Treated him like an animal. He was so beat up and scared that he was barely human. They made him do everything for them, whacked him all the time for no reason, took great pleasure in tormenting him. One of them dragged him off in the bushes and whatever they was doing, that boy screamed like no boy should ever scream. I'll never forget that scream as long as I live."

Zane was furious.

"They had themselves a little party, drinking and troubling that boy," the Greek continued. "When they all passed out, with the boy and me tied up, the boy tried to talk to me, but his whisper was so soft and his lip so busted, I could barely understand him. Something about getting home up to Ridgway, I think."

Zane's heart stopped. "Make yourself comfortable, old-timer. You're my guest here as long as you need." And with that, he picked himself up and hurried back to the house.

"Charlotte!" he yelled as he ran through the door. Finding her in the kitchen, he repeated the story, minus the horrific parts, to his wife.

"Do you think that could be Sean?" she asked, her heart bursting with fear and hope. Not a day went by that she didn't think about her missing brother.

"Impossible to say, but I reckon it could be. That's what I'm going to find out!" Zane exclaimed.

He knew there were four heartless, hardened killers awaiting him on this mission. He also knew that an innocent boy, maybe his relative, was being badly abused and needed help. He had no choice but to go. He could never again call himself a man if he left a boy, kin or no, in such horrible straits. Charlotte threw together some provisions while Zane assembled his weapons: a Winchester rifle and three loaded pistols. With some quick directions from the Greek, he was off.

"Be careful!" the Greek yelled after him. "Those four are killers!"

It was a shot in the dark, attempting to find five people in the vast wilderness. Fortunately, Zane was able to retrace the trail the Greek had taken as he walked from his campsite to the ranch. It was two full days of riding to the Vallecito, where he hoped to read signs and pick up the trail of his prey. Luck smiled on Zane toward twilight on the second day. Not only did he find the campsite the Greek had described, but the gang was still there as well.

Quickly, he formulated a plan. He needed to strike fast, and with complete surprise. He knew he could not prevail in a prolonged gunfight. The treachery the Greek told him of proscribed that these four deserved killing, no judge or jury required. There would be no warning or parley. Sticking his extra pistol in his belt, he took his horse's reins in his teeth, and with a pistol in one hand and the Winchester in the other, he spurred his horse to a gallop.

Approaching from the west, he burst into the camp with the sun at his back to blur their vision, yelling like a banshee. Zane had an additional advantage that he hadn't counted on, but was nonetheless grateful for. The four had been drinking heavily, possibly for several hours, and initially they moved like men stuck in amber. Stunned by the ferocious surprise attack, the outlaws struggled for their guns, but all too late. Zane emptied both rifle and pistol into their bodies with a marksman's accuracy. He tossed away the Winchester and drew one of his remaining pistols. It was unnecessary. They were all dead. Dismounting, he nevertheless checked each to make sure his work was done.

Where was the boy?

Zane walked in slow circles around the fire until he spotted marks in the dirt where someone had been dragged. There were spots of dried blood along the way. Following into the brush, he found a lifeless body. The boy was about fifteen. Covered in bruises and burn marks, he was hog-tied facedown with a noose around his neck that was tied to the rope around his wrists and ankles. His legs and arms were tied so tight that he must have been in intense pain. In his struggle to relieve the pain in his joints, he had strangled himself to death, just as his barbaric tormentors had planned.

Zane cleaned up the body as best he could. He didn't want Charlotte to see him like this. He wrapped the body in blankets and tied it off over the saddle of one of the four horses the gang had left behind. He left the men's bodies for the animals. They didn't deserve burying. He took the horses and gear with him, thinking they would help the Greek make a new start. The sale of this outfit would give him a fighting chance.

He found the Winchester where he had tossed it, picked it up and dusted it off, and reloaded it before sliding it into the scabbard attached to his horse's saddle. These four criminals were now dead and harmless, but Zane would be prepared for any others he might encounter on the trail home.

The trip back to the ZVH ranch, slow and plodding with four horses trailing behind him, took two full days. Zane rode up to the barn, where he was met by the astonished Greek. He handed him the rope to the string of horses and said, "They're all yours." Then he reached into his saddlebag and handed him his St. Christopher statue.

Now came the agonizing task that Zane had dreaded for two days. He unloaded the boy's body and laid it out in the barn. Charlotte had heard his arrival and rushed in. When she saw the boy-size body wrapped in blankets on the barn floor, she gasped and stopped in horror, drawing both hands in front of her mouth. Zane rushed over to take her in his arms, trying to hold her back. But she fought through, knelt beside the body, and frantically peeled the blankets from around the head, tears running down her cheeks. She looked at the face for the longest time, making not a sound. It was as though she had stopped breathing at all. Then, slowly, she replaced the blankets, stood, dusted her dress, and seemed to compose herself. She looked squarely at Zane. “That poor boy deserves to be buried right,” she said solemnly, “but it’s not my brother.” And then she turned and walked out of the barn, into the sunlight and back toward the house.

7

GOLD RUSH

Nothing, save tornados and earthquakes, can change a town so quickly and profoundly as word of a gold discovery and the consequent rush of adventurers seeking their fortune against all odds. The Sutter's Mill find in California in 1849 drew more than 300,000 people to an area that had previously been sparsely populated and had no infrastructure to support the enormous surge in population. Housing, supply lines, sanitary conditions, and law and order were pushed beyond capacity when the gold was found. A town like Durango would go from a population of 4,000 to 20,000 almost overnight, with more on the way daily.

That is exactly what happened when a major vein was found in the mountains north of Dolores, west of Durango. The Long Shot Mine hit a major deposit that would eventually yield $15 million in gold. It is one of the most iconic and cherished images among those who long remembered the Old West, what gold fever was truly like in those days. Hordes rushed into town from all the corners of the globe. Rushing toward imagined riches, they supplied at Vanderhorn's store and stable, got booze and rides at Strickland's saloons, and then headed for altitude in the quest for fame and fortune. Some would work themselves to death, most would quit in empty-handed despair, in greater poverty than when they arrived, and only a few would make the big find. Such is the calculus of gold fever.

As sure as night follows day, the seven deadly sins find a gold-rush town. Pride, greed, wrath, envy, lust, gluttony, and sloth found fertile soil among the desperate souls crowded together in a small town, with so few winners and so many losers. Robbery, theft, rape, and the like became a common occurrence in this once-peaceful community. Bad as things were on a day in July of 1878, they were about to get worse.

Trey Atkins and his gang approached Main Street on horseback, six across and daring anyone to get in their way. They rode deliberately and full of intimidation, like the cavalrymen that they were. Having served under Jeb Stuart in the war, they refused to accept defeat when Lee surrendered. They headed west, determined to keep the war going at every opportunity. They had no intent to engage in the backbreaking work of panning and mining for gold. From experience in other gold towns, they had honed their strategy of letting suckers do the hard work of bringing the gold aboveground, and then robbing them, either in their camps or on the trails to town. They only killed if necessary, and tried to rob only Yankees if possible, fancying themselves as nineteenth-century Robin Hoods. They would lay low in Durango with ears to the ground. When they would get wind of gold on the move, Atkins would announce that it was time to "stake a claim," and then they would set out to victimize some poor mining soul.

The Atkins gang became so proficient at their highwaymen ways that they came to the attention of Bart Strickland, who had already been benefiting from the gold rush by two means. First, he led a small band of highwaymen of his own, who found themselves competing with the Atkins gang robbing the miners, except Strickland's gang was clearly losing the competition. Second, he was running a crooked assay office where his rigged scales were cheating miners twenty cents on every dollar assayed. It was a sweet business, but it was drying up, much to Strickland's dissatisfaction.

Sheriff Dawson did his best to keep ahead of the crime surge, as the town doubled in size on a weekly basis. In his forties with graying temples and a slight limp, Dawson had been chosen as sheriff in Durango due to his prior successes in Texas and Kansas. He needed to draw on all of that previous experience, because in Durango at that time, he was outnumbered and outgunned. His wife had begged him to give up law enforcement for a safer and more peaceful life, but he wasn't ready just yet.

"Seen this before," the sheriff stated matter-of-factly to Otto Vanderhorn, Zane and Charlotte's oldest son. Dawson lit his pipe and took a seat in front of the jail on Main Street, nonchalantly laying a shotgun across his lap as he sat. "Unless we do something, it's just a matter of time before this blows up like the dynamite they're using up in the mines. Too much room for trouble. Too much competition and frustration all in one place. I can't be everywhere, and soon enough folks start taking matters into their own hands: gangs, fights, shootouts, vigilantes. Hard to control once it starts."

"Well," Otto replied thoughtfully, "let me know if I can help. But if it's all the same to you, I've seen enough trouble for a while. I won't back down from it, but I'll avoid it if I can."

Dawson was puzzled by Otto's less than enthusiastic support. He knew Otto had recently returned to the valley from serving in the army. What he couldn't know was that Otto had served in an ultra-secret elite force called the Ghosts. Reporting directly to Ulysses S. Grant while he was a general and then president, this squad was known only to Grant and fellow members. They had run special ops for Grant during the war, so successfully that the special unit was continued into his presidency. Under orders from Grant himself, they had gone undercover into the South to assassinate those who conspired with John Wilkes Booth to kill President Lincoln, whom Grant held in high esteem. They had forayed into Mexico to put down border troubles, and they had even been dispatched to the Barbary Coast to rescue captives from the pirates.

Otto had resigned his commission with honors and returned to Durango for a more peaceful life, or so he thought.

Bart Strickland didn't at all cotton to his business being hurt by the Atkins gang. But these were six tough hombres who would clearly cause anyone who crossed them to pay a great price. Clearly, he needed to make a move, but it needed to be the right move or it could be his last. So he waited.

Then, Teaspoon Weatherby was found shot to death. Teaspoon was over sixty, having spent forty years in the West seeking a fortune he never found. Short and bony, with wild gray hair and an unkept beard and clothes, he had a heart of gold, though not the kind he could never find in the mountains and streams. Everyone in the valley saw him as a beloved eccentric uncle figure. He had a signature whistle that told everyone Teaspoon was near, a whistle that became more difficult over the years as his teeth began to desert him. Teaspoon was missing his right ear—cut off by the Apache during his time as a captive. Fortunately for Teaspoon, his captivity had come to an end when some cowboys came upon him and his captors, and, in no small measure of generosity and even some compassion, traded two horses and a Henry rifle in exchange for his release. One of the first prospectors in the valley, even before the rush, he never struck it rich. His efforts at panning for gold yielded small amounts here and there over the years, barely enough to feed himself. A kind soul with no family to speak of, he made a habit of dropping off a little gold dust to the Sisters of Charity at the mission whenever he had a find, to help out the orphans in their care.

Teaspoon was found on the trail halfway between his camp and town, shot in the back. His pack mules were found nearby, undisturbed. Robbery wasn't the motive, it appeared. Maybe frustrated bandits shot him because he had nothing of value to rob. Or maybe there was another reason, who's to say? Dead men tell no tales, as the saying goes, especially on a trail in the middle of nowhere. In any case, Teaspoon's body was discovered by two of Strickland's men, who subsequently brought the corpse to town and presented it to the sheriff. They told Dawson that Teaspoon was barely alive when they found him, and before he died had muttered two words: "Atkins bastards."

Word quickly spread around town that Teaspoon was murdered. Although skeptical of the story, Sheriff Dawson set out to talk to Trey Atkins. He came upon all six of the Atkins gang as they were dismounting in front of the Broken Mustang. When they saw the sheriff approaching, they quickly spread wide and flanked him to left and right.

"Atkins," the sheriff began, "Teaspoon's body was found up in the canyon, shot in the back. I have reason to believe your men might—"

Before he could finish the sentence, Skinny Lockhart cleared leather and let loose a barrage at Dawson. The sheriff returned fire and a furious shootout commenced with the six outlaws. Hit twice, Dawson ducked behind the protection of a water trough as a hail of bullets rained down around him. The shots echoed through the now empty streets as the gang repositioned for the kill. Dawson was pinned and hopeless. Suddenly, two loud shots roared over his head in the direction of his assailants, and two of the gang hit the ground almost simultaneously. Seemingly out of nowhere, Otto Vanderhorn appeared on horseback, like a ghost, although to Sheriff Dawson he must have seemed more like an avenging angel. Having hit the two Atkins men at full gallop, Vanderhorn next leapt off his mount in one motion, with Winchester in hand, kicking his horse to safety as he dropped to the dusty street, and joining the sheriff behind the slim cover of the water trough.

"That should improve the odds a bit," Otto said to the fearfully wounded sheriff, who was never in his life so happy to see anyone.

But it was still four against two, and Otto and Dawson were in a precarious position. If the Atkins gang moved to their flank or rear, the water trough would offer no protection and they would be sitting ducks.

Otto rolled out to his left quickly. Never leaving the prone position, he caught Lockhart full in the chest with a blast from his Winchester, then rolled back before a return volley could be fired in his direction. Three down, he thought.

Sheriff Dawson was bleeding badly. One bullet had lodged in his right thigh, and the other had struck his left shoulder, when suddenly a third shattered his right elbow. Gamely, he tried to hold a gun, but he no longer could.

Three against one, Otto considered. The odds had suddenly gotten worse, and not only that, but the three he was against were well positioned behind barrels and wagons in front of the Broken Mustang, with no way for Otto to get a clean shot.

It looked desperate, and then came one of the most improbable turn of events in the history of Durango.

Bart Strickland walked out the swinging doors of the Broken Mustang behind the three remaining Atkins men, casual as could be, a chaw of tobacco bulging one cheek. He calmly raised a six-gun in each hand and shot two of the gang in the back as they peered forward, looking intently for a shot at Otto and Dawson. Stunned, Trey Atkins rose to his feet with a pistol in each hand. Reeling about like a drunken man, thinking himself surrounded, he blindly unleashed in all directions a barrage of lead from both hands, whereupon in the next moment, he raced off, leapt onto the back of his black roan, and sprinted out of town.

Otto and the sheriff looked on in astonishment.

Strickland walked over with an evil twinkle in his eye, spit a thick stream of tobacco juice into the dirt, and boasted, "Just a good citizen doing my duty to come to the aid of law enforcement in their time of need," his voice dripping with irony and sarcasm.

And there it was, the one time in the history of Durango that the Vanderhorns and Stricklands worked together, more or less. By plan or by chance, Strickland had rid himself of a pesky competitor gang, with Otto Vanderhorn having done most of the heavy lifting, and Sheriff Dawson having provided, well, you might call it the stamp of legality and just plain justice.

Dawson survived his wounds, but the shattered elbow in his shooting arm effectively brought to an end his days in law enforcement. And for that, his wife was actually grateful.

And that's also how Otto Vanderhorn, with no desire to do so, inherited the job of sheriff after Dawson's forced early retirement, and went on to become the most famous lawman in the history of Durango.

8

HENRY DRUMMOND

Jimmy O'Brien was a broken man. His body, mind, and spirit had been crushed by the Civil War. He had escaped his native Ireland with a dream of prosperity and a new life in America, but what he found was close to hell on earth. Conscripted into the Union army soon after landing in New York City, he was ill prepared and poorly trained when he was immediately sent to the front lines as a private in a newly formed infantry unit. Rushed in as a combat reinforcement, he fought in the Battle of the Wilderness, where he witnessed carnage beyond measure. Twenty-seven thousand soldiers were killed or wounded in three days of fighting, and he was at the center of the horror. Soon afterward, he was captured, becoming one of thousands of Union soldiers sent to the notorious prison in Georgia known as Andersonville. It was there that his spirit broke.

When the war ended, he was one of the few survivors of what was, by any definition, a concentration camp. Tens of thousands of soldiers were crowded into a stockade fence enclosure that covered twenty-six acres. The conditions were deplorably inhuman: inadequate shelter, minimal food rations, tainted water, open latrines, no medical care of any kind. More than thirteen thousand Union soldiers, one-third of those imprisoned at Andersonville, died in captivity. As the months passed, malnutrition caused O'Brien's body to feed on itself, damaging his organs, muscles, and nervous system. He was riddled with parasites. His brain suffered from lack of proper care and nutrition and sleep. He was rescued when the war ended, but he never fully recovered from the trauma he had suffered at the hands of the Confederate guards.

In a condition that lingered somewhere between alive and dead, and like so many others at the end of the war with no home to return to, he headed West on a horse that by appearances had lived every bit as hard a life as had Jimmy O'Brien had. Both were bags of skin and bones, with listless, lifeless eyes and vacant, hollow expressions. They made a sorry pair who looked as if they would be blown away by a gentle breeze.

This was the sad image that arrived on Main Street in Durango one hot summer day several years after the war. Jimmy dismounted from his horse, tied it off near a water trough, and gamely limped up the street to get himself a drink wherever one might be available. As he rounded the corner of Main and Maple, he froze in place, the air rushing out of his lungs. Had he not been numbed, psychologically and even physically, by what he saw, he would have realized he had slightly peed himself.

Before him, no more than forty feet away, stood the man Durango knew as Bart Strickland, but whom Jimmy O'Brien knew as Henry Drummond, the meanest son of a bitch of all the scoundrels who guarded the suffering Union prisoners in their agony at Andersonville.

The prison had always been bad, but as conditions in the South deteriorated, and the course of the war went against them, the citizenry struggled for food and necessities. With what little they had, there was none to spare for the Union prisoners, whom they targeted with the hateful wrath they felt for the likes of Grant and Sherman, the demons from the North who rained devastation down upon the South. It seemed that the guards were picked for their sadistic viciousness because of the way they treated the prisoners. A lack of provisions was one thing, but the guards appeared to actively enjoy making the prisoners' lives as horrific as possible. In short, the way Jimmy O'Brien saw it, they were the cruelest, most heartless, most vicious torturers the South could summon up. The prisoners hated those guards with a fervor that would burn for the rest of their lives. The most hated of all was Henry Drummond.

Drummond took demonic pleasure in tormenting the prisoners. Inside the perimeter of the stockade was a small, low fence called the deadline. Twenty feet from the actual barricade, it served as a buffer keeping the prisoners away from the wall. Armed guards were stationed on the wall at various intervals, and prisoners who crossed the line would be shot on sight with no warning. Drummond relished an assignment to one or another of the guard towers, and he was infamous for having the most kills from those high perches. It was known among the prisoners that, if nobody crossed the line, Drummond might shoot someone who ventured even close to the deadline, just for the evil enjoyment of executing the defenseless. At times, he would throw food just inside the deadline to entice the starving men into the shooting zone. He even went so far as to set up fights between a pair of starving prisoners over a bit of food ration. Three of O'Brien's closest friends died at the hand of this monster, and to Jimmy, Drummond was evil incarnate.

Now, only a few years later, here stood Jimmy O'Brien on an open street in the middle of Durango, a decade and two thousand miles away from that horrible place, believing he faced his tormentor. He had seen that face in his nightmares for all of those difficult years. Like most of the men who suffered in Andersonville, he had vowed to kill Drummond if the opportunity ever presented itself. Time changes the face of a person, but some less than others, and O'Brien swore Drummond was still recognizable after all these years.

Shaking so hard his pants started to fall down, O'Brien reached into his belt and pulled out the service revolver he had kept after the war, cocked the hammer back, and yelled, *"Henry Drummond, you son of a bitch!"* All of the people conducting their affairs on Main Street that day, including Strickland, turned almost simultaneously in the direction of the voice. As Strickland turned, O'Brien's first shot rang out. The myths of the West tend to portray gunfighters as deadeye marksmen instantly killing their foes with a single shot from great distances, but that's not how it really was. This gunfight progressed in the real world, not the world of legend.

As it was, O'Brien's first shot was high and to the right, shattering a lampstand. Clumsily swinging his pistol to adjust the trajectory, he fired off a second shot that flew wide to the left, where it hit a luckless stray dog drinking water from a muddy puddle. Strickland now returned fire, but his first shot merely shattered the barbershop window to the left of his target. Already overwhelmed with nerves and with the sinking reality that he had just lost the advantage of surprise, the poor Irishman dissolved into pure panic, allowing Strickland to take just an instant, barely a second, to steady his aim. His second shot nicked O'Brien in the leg. The Irishman wildly fired two more errant shots harmlessly into the ground as he winced and instinctively reached down to grab his leg.

At that moment, for some strange reason, both men paused. For Jimmy O'Brien, it was because there suddenly came the terrifying realization that, in his sorry financial straits, he had just uselessly discharged the last two of the few bullets he'd had in his possession, and his gun was now empty. Strickland seemed to realize it too. He smiled broadly, and with his right arm extended rigidly, pistol in hand, he proceeded to stride confidently right up to the now defenseless attacker, who helplessly fell backward into a seated position on the boardwalk. When Strickland got to within about five feet, he carefully aimed at O'Brien's chest and blew a hole that went right through the former Union soldier's heart.

Having heard the shots, Sheriff Vanderhorn arrived soon thereafter, the air still thick with the smell of gunpowder when he got there. Strickland laid down his gun and raised his hands. The sheriff secured the gun and sent for the doctor, but O'Brien was as dead as could be. A quick questioning of the numerous townsfolk who witnessed the whole thing clearly indicated that Strickland had acted in self-defense.

"The stranger pulled on Strickland; he had no choice," was the consensus. "The feller weren't right in his head, Sheriff," one of the eyewitnesses reported. "Called Mr. Strickland here by name of Drummond or some such."

"That so?" the sheriff asked, looking around, steely-eyed, at each of the other witnesses, who all nodded in agreement.

But as Strickland retrieved his weapon, Vanderhorn was suspiciously curious. "Why do you suppose he called you Drummond?"

Strickland sneered. "Musta mistook me for somebody else." He holstered his gun, sent a wild spit of dark brown tobacco juice in the direction of the dead man, and walked away.

9

THE STRIKE

Gold has such a unique hold over the imaginations of men, sometimes over entire human cultures, that it often outshines other matters in importance. The fact is, while gold was the target of fortune seekers in the Animas Valley in the final decades of the nineteenth century, the area was filled with countless other treasures in the ground. Along with gold and silver, the mountains rimming the valley, and on up to higher altitudes, held large deposits of iron ore, copper, zinc, lead, and especially coal. As the industrial revolution transformed the American economy, the soaring demand for metals created a boom in southwest Colorado. Enterprising men established mines at any spot with favorable probabilities of yielding metals and coal, and more often than not these were successful. Geology was an increasingly sophisticated field, and those who utilized this emerging science found fortunes were to be made, even if gold was never found. More than fifty mines sprang up within a day's ride from Durango City Hall, and the town became the epicenter of the mining boom.

Men who had already made fortunes in manufacturing and railroads and commodities back East set up footholds in the burgeoning mining industry in the area, in the quest for even greater fortunes. Mining claims were secured as quick as could be by these competing captains of industry, who raced each other to see who could create the bigger fortune. Competition was fierce for mining experts, operations managers, geologists, and the like. Labor, however, was plentiful. As the rest of the country struggled through an economic depression, hundreds of workers gravitated to Durango where work, as grueling as it was, was nevertheless abundantly available in the mines. Mine owners, aware of the imbalance, secured all the labor they wanted at the paltry price of three dollars a day. At those wage levels, a mine owner could easily become a millionaire quickly, while his workers barely scratched out an existence working eight-hour days.

Despite the fortunes being made, some of the mine owners saw the oversupply of labor as an opportunity to further increase their profits. At a meeting in the dining room at their exclusive hotel in the Enclave, their neighborhood, they decided to increase the workday from eight hours to ten, with no increase in wages. With so many workers available, they felt that any who didn't accept the new terms could be easily replaced. The vote was not unanimous. Industrial barons Victor Altman and Philip Jefferson, emerging as leaders of an informal consortium of mine owners, persuaded two other owners to vote with them. The sole holdout was Cornelius Bailey. When the vote was in, Bailey lowered his head, overcome by the sadness he sensed would come from this greedy move. But even he couldn't predict the trouble it would bring.

"How much wealth does a man need?" he asked his colleagues rhetorically. They snickered in response.

After summoning their foremen to spread the word about the new work rules, the mine owners walked out of the hotel and went directly to their newly built mansions in the Enclave. Their homes were built side by side in a half-moon configuration at the base of the hill that led up to the mines. Facing west, these homes had a perfect view of the glorious sunsets, as the evening sun sank below the peaks of the mountains that gave them their wealth. Of late, the view was being tainted by rickety shacks and hovels that were being put up by the mine workers to provide meager shelter for them and their families. Quietly, the owners had approved a plan to knock down all the pitiful structures one day soon, while the workers were toiling in the mines.

As word spread of the new work schedule, enraged miners poured into the streets. Union talk had already begun, and this money grab was the last straw. Angus McGee, who led the organizing movement, rallied the miners together, proclaiming, "If we are ever going to stand for ourselves, we must stand now!"

Sensing both opportunity and desperation, the miners banded together under his leadership in a way that stunned the owners and seized the moment. McGee determined to take the initiative in a bold and unexpected way. He gathered the workers' leaders together and laid out his plan.

"The owners think they are going to lock us out of the mines. They don't yet realize they are the ones being locked out!" he announced. That very night, eight hundred miners fanned out in a coordinated plan. A contingent went to each mine, overpowered the startled night watchmen, and secured access to the mines for themselves and no others. A larger group proceeded to the hovel camp above the Enclave, where they quickly built barricades and fires, making the road impassable. Having gone to bed with visions of even greater profits dancing in their heads, the stunned owners awoke to find a ragtag band of poorly armed workers had seized the high ground above their ring of gaudy mansions, and worse, they had effectively shut down their entire operation.

Durango's other citizens also awoke that morning to the stunning news of the revolt that had gone up against the mining companies. As in any labor conflict, scores of the populace sympathized with either side, and inevitably some were sympathetic to both sides. Many had a sympathy for the struggling strikers. Others feared loss of business from the shutdown. Everyone had an opinion, including both Sheriff Vanderhorn and Bart Strickland.

When Otto Vanderhorn learned of the occupation on Camp Hill, he rode out to see for himself. Arriving at the crest of the hill, he found a six-foot barricade had been hastily built across the road, and it was there he was greeted by Angus McGee. Vanderhorn looked around the fortifications, ramshackle in their construction, perhaps, but formidable to anyone who might try to breach. He nodded to several of the miners he recognized, and said to their leader, "So, what next, Angus?"

McGee explained the grievances of the miners as Vanderhorn listened sympathetically. After hearing out the de facto labor leader, he said, "Let me talk to the owners and see what I can do."

The sheriff returned to the Enclave and entered the dining room at the hotel, where the owners were having breakfast, caught up in frantic arguments about what they saw as nothing less than a coup attempt, plain and simple.

Victor Altman led the agitated capitalists, yelling, "Let's wire the governor and get the military here! We'll show those sons of bitches what's what!"

Cornelius Bailey, as was his wont, tried to be the voice of reason and compromise, but his fellow owners were not men who were accustomed to such, and he got nowhere. Altman sent word to the governor, who would shortly respond by sending six officials to monitor the situation. No matter how much Otto Vanderhorn tried, he couldn't get either side to budge. So, the Camp Hill mining strike dragged on for days, weeks, and months, and during that time, the economy of Durango crashed to a full stop. The miners foraged for scraps of food and took to hunting in the surrounding hillsides, while some of them received meager supplies from sympathetic townsfolk. The two sides had reached a stalemate.

Bart Strickland was a keen observer of the struggle around him. Not one to let a crisis go to waste, he saw an opening. He knew he would never be accepted by the owners under any circumstances—he was certainly "not their kind"—so there was nothing to gain by siding with them. They might avail themselves of his services to end the strike, and they would likely pay handsomely for those services, but they would discard him as soon as they could thereafter. The strikers, on the other hand, were hopeless, uneducated, easily led, and increasingly desperate. A union would give him a base that would help him forward his ambitions. In the fifth month of the standoff, Bart Strickland approached the miners' camp and shared his plans with Angus McGee. After hearing the plan, McGee thought Strickland was either mad or a genius, maybe a little of both. But Angus knew he had to do something to break the stalemate, as his people were getting restless and beginning to lose hope in the cause. So, with fear and trepidation, he agreed to Strickland's devious plan.

The next morning, McGee rode the hundred yards down the hill from the barricade to the Enclave under a white flag. As Strickland had instructed, McGee advised the owners that the mouth of each mine they owned had been set with dynamite. If their demands were not met, they would begin to blow up the mines. The owners were aghast at this audacious move. As Angus turned back up the hill, he called out to the stunned owners, "This is to show we are serious. We will not back down."

A minute later, a thundering explosion was heard from the direction of the mines. The owners recoiled in terror, not knowing whose mine had been destroyed. The air in the lobby of the Enclave Hotel was filled with the angst and terror of men who loved money and were watching the sources of it being destroyed before their eyes. In a while there was another far-off explosion, then another. The bombardment was having exactly the terrifying effect Strickland expected it to. The owners were beside themselves. An urgent telegraph was sent to the governor, and several days later a military detachment was dispatched by train to put down the rebellion.

In the days that followed, Bart Strickland continued his psychological warfare on the mine owners. From time to time, he had miners set off large quantities of dynamite at various spots around the mines, but never actually damaging them. Periodically, Angus McGee would send an emissary to the owners to see if they would negotiate, but they wouldn't budge. Finally, knowing that the strikers were running out of time and patience, Strickland played his ace in the hole. He sent a messenger requesting the owners to assemble for a parley on the front steps of the hotel, facing the miners' camp. When they came outside they saw a fully loaded wagon at the top of the hill facing them. Bart Strickland was standing next to it, grinning. Wordlessly, Strickland loosed the brake and set the wagon hurtling down the hill, as flames began to engulf its cargo. The wagon picked up speed as it raced downhill toward the stunned owners and their mansion enclave. As they stood frozen in shock, the dynamite-laden wagon crashed directly into Victor Altman's mansion.

The front facade of the house imploded from the impact, followed by a massive explosion that shook the ground and blew out several windows on the other mansions. In what seemed like but an instant, Altman's home was fully engulfed in fire, flames shooting out of the doors and windows, the structure collapsing in on itself. Too shocked to speak or move, the owners looked up the hill to see the cheering miners rolling another overloaded wagon into place.

Just as the miners were about to level another mansion, a bugle call was heard, announcing the arrival of the army unit that the governor had dispatched. Over one hundred crack troops, with long rifles, four cannons, and a Gatling gun, quickly formed a military perimeter along the base of the hill and in front of the Enclave. The tide had turned.

The contingent was led by Colonel Lucien Trahane, a Civil War hero who was known to be an excellent soldier, as well as a stone-cold killer when such action was required. By reputation, he was a man to be feared. Following the governor's orders, he positioned his men for an assault on the sorry defenses of the miners. Just as the attack was about to sound, Sheriff Vanderhorn approached on horseback under a white flag. Descending from the mine camp, he stopped on the road, about halfway into the no-man's-land between the two sides. Colonel Trahane rode out alone to meet him.

"Welcome to Durango, Lucien," Otto said with a smile.

Lucien reached out his right hand to shake, and as Otto responded in kind, their two wrists were exposed, each bearing the tattoo of the Ghosts, the military unit in which they had served together under President Grant.

"Quite a pickle we got here," Trahane observed. "What do you propose?"

"I think we need to apply some leverage," the sheriff responded. With that, they devised a plan to diffuse the white-hot tension and, perhaps, bring an end to the strike.

The sheriff went to the miners and asked if they would be agreeable to go back to the eight-hour day at the same wage, letting them know that their option was a ferocious attack from the army, in which many of them were likely to die. He found them agreeable, and he relayed that information to the colonel. Trahane, in turn, told the owners that the miners were agreeable to a settlement at the previous pay scale. Since the miners were agreeable to end the strike, the colonel informed them he could, by order of his superiors, no longer attack them and would soon return with his troops to Denver. With their eyes on the wagons set atop the hill facing their homes, and at the prospect of being again defenseless, the owners agreed and the strike was ended.

The cooperative efforts of the miners laid the foundation for the start of the Western Miners Union. And of all things, Bart Strickland became a hero to the miners while staying largely behind the scenes, risking nothing of his own. Yet he had made a large group of friends that he confidently believed would be available to him in the future, whenever he needed them. Cornelius Bailey became the leader of the mine owners when Victor Altman, his mansion destroyed and his power of influence erased, sold his properties to the others and went back East.

Bailey championed better working conditions for the miners because, as he said often, "It's the right thing to do."

10

THE MASSACRE

Henry Miller was a pious man, a devout Calvinist who looked at his life as a mystery written by someone else and over which he grudgingly accepted he had no control. He took life as it came because he didn't believe he had any say in the matter. His life was one unintentional event after another, having no seeming direction or purpose because his particular brand of Christianity stated that he had no choice but to live the life he was predestined for.

He wandered from school to job to town with no apparent plan or design, because to him it seemed there was no point in having one. His marriage to a woman named Margaret just seemed like the thing to do, a decision he didn't resent over the years, although it gave him no particular enthusiasm, either.

It was just a series of circumstances that brought him to the West, where his diligent and compliant nature brought him to the attention of the local authorities. Accordingly, Miller quickly gained appointment to the position of Indian agent, responsible for the members of the Ute tribe that lived to the west of Durango. Never was there a more unqualified person given authority over a more unwilling populace.

With no real direction or support from the government as to how to proceed, Miller used the Ohio town he grew up in as a template for the community he wanted to establish. Believing that the Utes' days as warriors and hunters were over, he endeavored to turn this proud group of nomadic hunter-gatherers, as sociologists would later categorize them, into farmers, agrarians, a life that neither the Utes, nor Miller himself, knew anything about. The policy at the time, deeply flawed from its very inception, was, "To save the man you have to kill the Indian."

Whatever the intention, the indigenous people didn't want, or need, to be saved by the white man, nor would they allow their venerable heritage to be killed. Constant tension, economic failure, and unrelenting impoverishment kept the reservation lands in a continual state of turmoil. As rumors circulated that other tribes were leaving their reservations and either fighting their captivity or, like Chief Joseph and the Nez Perce, attempting to flee through Montana to Canada, the Utes were pitted against the increasing number of white settlers, making for a volatile situation.

The lighted match arrived one day on a black horse. Bart Strickland rode to introduce himself to Miller and offer his help.

"Miller, you've got your hands full here, and little experience in these matters to fall back on. I've been friends with the Ute since I was a boy. Chief Ouray of the mountain Ute is a boyhood friend," he lied. "I sure would like to see these folks well took care of," he said, extending an assuring hand. Miller, desperate for a rescue from this sinking enterprise, enthusiastically embraced Strickland's offer of help, and in doing so launched one of the most disastrous partnerships in the history of Colorado.

Strickland knew that the army delivered an irregular flow of supplies to Miller, who as the Indian agent was responsible for distributing them to the tribe. Little attention was paid to what came in, nor was there any formal accounting or record keeping of how it was distributed. Miller was authorized to make purchases of food and equipment from his government expense account to supplement the deliveries that came irregularly.

Strickland won his confidence and insinuated himself into the entire process. It was a gold mine.

"Don't you worry, I'll take care of all that," Strickland promised with a smile. He proceeded to rob the resources of the Ute reservation blind, leaving the tribe with barely enough to survive. Food, tools, blankets, clothing: Anything of use, and of value, could be found on the black market from Greely to Telluride, leaving the Utes for whom those vital supplies were intended cold, hungry, more destitute than ever—and angry.

On one point there would remain some dispute, even to this day. Some say Miller was a willing accomplice in this scheme; others say he knew nothing of it, a hapless dupe out of his league. Perhaps he knew but was too intimidated to stop it. Or he just didn't care. But in all likelihood, it was a combination of all of those.

Finally, the Utes could take no more abuse. Chief Guero led a contingent of twenty warriors to the agency office to confront

Miller and demand the resources and supplies that had been promised them in the treaty.

Miller and Strickland came out on the office porch to confront Chief Guero and his warriors. They were soon backed by five white men who worked at the agency.

"Miller, we want our food, our tools, feed for our horses, clothes, all the things that your worthless treaties promised us. We see these come here but never make it to our lodges," the chief said with a steely resolve. "You will give us what is ours *now*, or we will take our complaint to the army, directly to the superintendent at Fort Meriwether."

Miller considered how to answer the chief, until Strickland stepped forward, looked Chief Guero in the eye, and said, "Chief, you can take your complaint and stick it up your ass!"

No one knows who shot first, but the yard exploded in a hail of gunfire. Years of abuse and rage boiled over into a vicious attack. Miller, Strickland, and their men ran back into the agency offices seeking cover, as the Utes fanned out across the yard and surrounded the building. It was only a matter of time before the white men would be overwhelmed. All seven were killed within minutes.

An arrow launched from Chief Guero struck Strickland in the chest, and then another. He struggled to pull one out as he felt the air from his lungs bursting out of the hole. His mouth filled with blood and he fell to the ground. His vision began to blur as the bloodcurdling shrieks of the victorious warriors began to fade from his hearing. He began to feel his soul lifting out of his body as it departed this world and entered the hereafter. There was no warm bright light for him, only the deepest imaginable darkness. His immersion in nothingness was soon interrupted by a presence, then another, then another. He slowly began to recognize the creatures as the souls of all those he had wronged in his evil life. Suddenly these beings that he could sense but not see exploded in ferocity and began to tear at his very soul, devouring him in a frenzy that belied the damage he had done to them. As his mutilated soul began to disintegrate into the nothingness that awaits all evil men, his last thought was of Charlotte McClintock.

The Utes next set fire to the agency building, which quickly burned to the ground. They piled all of the stores—the equipment, the tools, the food—from the agency's supply barn into wagons, later to be transported to their villages where they rightfully belonged. All the horses were taken too, as compensation, Chief Guero proclaimed, for that which they had been cheated of for so long. And yet, the chief gave two orders that his warriors respected: No women or scalps would be taken.

"We have not done this for any reason but justice," the chief announced. "We do not want to escalate this beyond what these here deserve for what they have done to our people. An eye for an eye, as the white man says. I hope that is enough."

But it wasn't. With her husband dead, his remains somewhere in the ashes of the Indian agency complex, Maggie Miller walked for three days until a wrangler found her and brought her to town.

Word of the massacre infuriated the townsfolk, none more so than Nathaniel Harrison. Harrison, formerly a colonel in the Union army, had made a name for himself in the Civil War as a cavalryman, leading bold charges against the Rebs at Gettysburg and Cold Harbor. He had come West with his family after the war, hoping to go into ranching, to spend his remaining days in a peaceful and pastoral setting. But tragically, his wife and one of his daughters were killed in an Indian raid on the wagon train that had carried them across the plains of western Kansas. An arrow in his left leg left him with a noticeable limp. The story Maggie Miller told of the massacre brought back those awful memories, and, to Harrison's way of thinking, cried out for revenge.

Harrison sent messengers to every corner of the Animas Valley with news of the horrible atrocities of what some, if they had only known more about the actual circumstances, might easily have regarded as a justifiable act on the part of the Utes. This was of no matter to Harrison.

With the army garrison at Fort Meriwether undermanned, largely due to deployments of troops chasing Geronimo and the Apache in New Mexico, Harrison formed a militia of his own. Nearly four hundred men formed the First La Plata Militia, sworn to avenge the deaths of the corrupt Indian agent and his accomplices. Leading the charge were Josh, Jake, and Caleb Strickland, fresh from burying their father.

Hearing of the campaign about to begin, Sergeant Harmon of Fort Meriwether, along with six soldiers, accompanied the militia to offer what strategic support they could, if necessary. For five days they trailed a large party of Indians as it moved north and west, away from Durango.

Gabriel Foster, a buffalo soldier and scout, voiced his concerns to Sergeant Harmon. "Sarge, those ain't war-party tracks. Looks like just a village moving about; women, children, animals too."

On the sixth day, scouts returned with word that the Indians had been spotted making camp along Cripple Creek, just to the north. Harrison laid his plan out before his assembled troops.

"No quarter, no mercy, no prisoners!" he commanded.

They broke for the night and prepared for battle.

That evening, Harmon approached Harrison in his tent. "Harrison, there's a good chance that those aren't the Indians who attacked the agency. We need to check this out more before we act."

"Nonsense," Harrison replied, "we have our enemy before us and vengeance will be ours."

Harmon realized his band of six was no match for the militia that enthusiastically supported Harrison. Harmon recognized that this militia was in no way a legitimate military unit, but rather a ragtag bunch of low-life Indian-haters, brawlers, and malcontents for the most part. Harmon slept fitfully through the night in despair over what was to come.

In the morning, Nathaniel Harrison's militia formed a battle line across the creek from the sleeping camp. Ahead of them someone unfurled a flag of the Colorado territory. Napoleon Lafitte, who bragged that he had pirated with the Lafittes of New Orleans, hoisted a skull and crossbones flag on the end of a bayonet.

"Show these savages no more mercy than did they show our sons and daughters and fathers and mothers. No mercy, no prisoners," Harrison commanded, reiterating his orders of the previous day, and with that began one of the darkest days in the history of the West.

While Chief Guero and his band awoke in a quiet camp near Pagosa Springs fifty miles away, this innocent band of Utes, who had nothing to do with the deaths of Miller, Strickland, and the rest, awoke to pure carnage. With most of their young men off hunting, two hundred old men, women, and children were slaughtered to avenge the deaths of seven whites who had been stealing from the tribe, and profiting monstrously from that theft. One elder of the tribe came out of his tepee with an American flag in one hand and a copy of the Constitution in the other. Caleb Strickland knocked him to the ground, then scalped him alive with one stroke. He let him suffer in shock for a few minutes as blood ran down his forehead and into his eye sockets. Then Caleb deftly slit his throat as Harrison watched approvingly.

Harmon and the Fort Meriwether soldiers observed the unfolding massacre in horror from a distance. Harrison sent a messenger to their position.

"Sergeant Harmon, Colonel Harrison orders you to engage your men," the messenger stated.

"Harrison is no colonel," he replied. "This is madness, and we refuse to take part in the murder of innocent and unarmed women and children."

Harrison returned to Durango a conquering hero. He was the toast of the town for putting down the Indian rebellion that never was. And while Sergeant Harmon duly filed a report with his commander about the massacre at Cripple Creek, his commander saw Harrison's actions as necessary to address the ongoing, seemingly endless troubles with the Indians, and refused to take any steps. Privately, he was grateful that Harrison had done the dirty work that would likely have fallen to him eventually. Outraged, Harmon filed complaints in Denver and Washington about the senseless carnage at Cripple Creek, telling the newspapers and anyone else who would listen about the needless and immoral slaughter. His one-man campaign ended one morning when Harmon was found in the alley behind the Broken Mustang with a bullet in his forehead.

Nathaniel Harrison regaled in the role of the conquering hero. Many a time he would tell the story of the five hundred warriors his outnumbered men had killed in the raid, of their heroism and bravery under fire as they saved Colorado from the savages. In every story, he told of the fierce battle in which Caleb Strickland had fiercely fought the Indian chief to the death in hand-to-hand combat, when all he had actually done was kill a helpless old man. Caleb had made a big impression on him, enough so that he arranged for him to marry his daughter Abigail. Caleb and Abigail would have a long and awful marriage that produced beatings, infidelity, and bitter heartache, as well as two sons, Griff and Wade, spawn of two evil families that would carry their criminal legacy into the new century.

11

THE CAPTIVE

It is a matter of Old West history that part of the ongoing warfare between the natives and the settlers involved the taking of captives, a practice that actually predated the arrival of the white man. Captives proved useful for all sorts of reasons, including as slaves or laborers, for rape or as brides, as children being added to families, or even for target practice, human sacrifice, and forms of torture. There was no greater terror on the frontier than the thought of women and children being abducted and held forever in a harsh world under horrific circumstances, never to see their families again, and to endure conditions deemed worse than death.

The story of Cynthia Ann Parker is probably the most famous captive story of the West. She was kidnapped at ten years old and lived with the Comanche, to be rescued more than twenty years later by a squad of Texas Rangers led by Charles Goodnight. Hers was not the only such story, just the most famous. It was so popular because of an unspoken statement that it seemed to convey: Captives are still alive and need to be looked for! Most often, the folks taken captive were not alive, but the possibility brought precious hope to the families of those who were gone, and a cause célèbre to the wannabe heroes determined to free them. And when word came that a captive had been located, communities formed militias not simply to rescue them, but also to wreak vengeance on those who kidnapped them.

Such was the attitude of settlers in Colorado in the spring of 1880, when a mountain man wandered into Durango. He had wintered with Chief Ouray and the Ute tribe at a place called Boulder Gulch. He told the story of a white boy who was living with the Utes. Without any idea of the calamity he was about to ignite, he simply said, "The Utes call him Sings Like Wolf. But I think it's the Romney boy."

Word spread through the town like a flash flood. One day, years earlier, young Will Romney, who was fourteen years old at the time, was out tending cows on his family's small farm in Mormon Utah, and then he was gone without a trace. Everyone had assumed that he had been swept up by a Ute war party and, if still alive, was destined to a life of pain and suffering and degradation. Now and then a rumor would go around that he had been found, mutilated and disfigured, or worse. Other times, rumors circulated that his dead body had been found, but none of the rumors were ever substantiated. For five years his whereabouts were unknown.

Word that Will Romney might be in Boulder Gulch reached Caleb Strickland. With a mind as evil and cunning as his father

Bart's, he too saw an opportunity. Rumors abounded that Boulder Gulch, just east of Silverton, had a vein that was likely to contain gold. Some itinerant panners had actually found specks of color in the river. However, that region hadn't been fully investigated because, in another treaty with Chief Ouray, that land was given to the Utes. The irony gave Caleb Strickland headaches. A whole gold mine was waiting for him, he thought, if not for those damned Indians. There was not much he could do about it—unless, he reasoned—unless they were holding captives against their will, in which case it was his duty to rescue them! And if some, or all, of the Indians were killed in the effort, or run off, unfortunate as that would be, that was a small price to pay to return young Will to the loving arms of his ma. He laughed to himself at the beauty of his scheme.

The word went out on the streets and in the saloons that Will Romney had been located and the Stricklands were forming a posse to go rescue him as a matter of duty. Soon the town was caught up in the frenzy. Horses, weapons, and supplies were assembled. Caleb, Josh, and Jake Strickland, three brothers from the pit of hell who in later times might be called sociopaths, appointed themselves leaders of the crusade. Nearly a hundred and forty men prepared for the three-day journey to rescue Will Romney.

Sheriff Otto Vanderhorn got word of the upstart campaign and came out clearly against it. He even appealed directly to the Stricklands, but to no avail. Nor could the passions of the crowd be quieted, due in no small part to the fact that the Stricklands had made no secret that if the Utes were killed off there would be gold to be found in Boulder Gulch, and anyone who helped rescue Will Romney would be entitled to a share. Of course, they had no intention of sharing such a find.

Sheriff Vanderhorn approached the three Strickland boys in the run-down saloon their father had left them. The three were seated at a table, playing cards. They didn't look up as he approached, but each readied their pistol in case an opportunity arose to kill him. The Stricklands' hatred for Vanderhorns was never far below the surface. All any of them needed was a small excuse to shoot the sheriff right where he stood.

"Boys, I know what you are planning for Boulder Gulch and I can't let that happen," Otto stated directly. "If Will Romney is really up there, we need to do things the right way. Chief Ouray has always been very cooperative. I am going to contact the army and ask them to send a patrol up to the Utes and see what's what."

"No sir, Sheriff." Caleb looked up with a big smile on his face. "We can't take that chance. Who knows but that poor Will ain't staked out right now with flaming arrows being shot into his poor white body." The two other brothers giggled. "No sir, Sheriff. We can't wait for the army. They might be too late. We good citizens of Durango need to do our duty and rescue that boy. We ain't got a minute to lose."

Vanderhorn assessed the situation and quickly determined he was unlikely to sway the crowd from joining the evil plan. He backed out through the saloon doors slowly, as the three Stricklands continued with their devious plot to rescue Will Romney.

The problem was, Will didn't need rescuing at all, because he wasn't a captive.

When Will was fourteen years old he was a free spirit. He longed for adventure and was bored tending cows and doing tedious chores on his family's small farm on the Colorado-Utah border. His was a devout Mormon family. His mom, Georgia Romney, had birthed twelve children, nine who survived infancy. They had fled Ohio with other Mormons when the persecution there started. While most of their party went on to the Great Salt Lake, Georgia had become too weak to travel. So they settled on a small plot of rocky land on the western slopes of the Rockies, despite there being little water and few prospects there. His father, Joseph, was a well-educated man who had once taught at a university. Unfortunately, the subjects in which he was most knowledgeable and proficient had little to do with farming. Theirs was a miserable life, filled with intractable poverty and constant struggle. Will, the oldest surviving boy, carried much of the responsibility that overflowed from his parents' lack of skills in running a farm under such harsh circumstances.

One day a milk cow wandered off. Will set out to track it, when he found a small opening in the tangle of overgrown brush beyond the back end of their homestead land, and he pushed through it. To his astonishment, he came upon three young Ute warriors, all about his age, sitting around a small fire. One of the warriors noticed Will and quickly rose with bow in hand, as if prepared to slay the white boy. But Running Bear, their leader, stopped him. Will's and Running Bear's eyes met, and for a bit they stared at each other. Then, Running Bear gestured with an open hand for Will to sit with them around the fire. And so he did. Although they didn't speak each other's language, they were able to use hand signals and play-acting to communicate. The three were from the tribe of Chief Ouray, the great chief of the Utes. They spent their days hunting, fishing, riding horses, chasing buffalo, and having sex with Indian girls.

"What do you do?" they motioned.

Will replied, "I watch cows. It's boring," nodding in disgust.

The Utes picked up on Will's tone and gestured for him to join them.

Will was surprised and perplexed by the offer. He didn't want to just leave his parents, but this life was boring as hell. His parents needed his help, but he was also another mouth to feed. Besides, he was almost a man and needed to get out on his own. He knew if he went back to his parents, they would stop him and he would be back to farming and shoveling manure and tending cows. So, he took them up on their offer and he left with them. Kicking Deer, one of the young Utes, offered him a place on his horse, and Will's new life as a Ute warrior had begun. As they sped away, he let out an exhilarated howl. That's how he got the name Sings Like Wolf.

His five years with the Utes were pleasant, although not quite the playground Running Bear had promised. Yes, there had been horses and hunting and fishing, but there was also cold, hunger, and constantly moving as white men encroached more and more on Ute territory. He forgot his white man identity, almost entirely. He didn't see himself as Will Romney anymore. He was Sings Like Wolf, a member of the Ute. He even came to think first in Ute language and culture, and not in English, or in the ways of the settlers he had left behind. But as years passed, Will felt more and more guilty about leaving his family. Whenever whites approached the tribe, he made himself scarce, embarrassed that he might be discovered and have to explain himself.

Accordingly, Will did his best to keep his distance from an old-timer who wintered with the tribe, but months of isolation, largely huddled together in one place, made it impossible to completely avoid him. Will never spoke directly to the old man. He had no idea that his "captivity" had been so famous, nor did he realize that the old-timer could put two and two together, and that as a consequence, his cover had been blown.

But blown it was. The Stricklands were forming a solid militia to mount a rescue mission that was completely unnecessary, except if you were a white man wanting an excuse to steal gold from Indians. The troop mounted up, and with the three Stricklands in the lead, they headed up the Animas Canyon on their three-day trek to steal the gold out from under Chief Ouray.

Sheriff Vanderhorn understood the motivations of the Stricklands well enough to know that their plan, in reality, would have nothing to do with Will Romney. The Strickland family had done nothing but no good for more than thirty years and didn't likely, all-of-a-sudden-like, get religion and turn from their predictable ways. He, too, had heard the rumors of the gold in Boulder Gulch. He couldn't comprehend that the Stricklands might be so evil that they would kill a whole tribe of Utes on the chance that the gold rumors were true—or that they might be foolish enough to try. After all, they would be facing a whole tribe of formidable warriors who wouldn't go without a fight. The Durango militia was better armed than the Utes, but they would be significantly outnumbered—and outclassed in the art of war. What chance would they have? Vanderhorn figured they must be counting on the element of surprise and confusion. He was convinced they were planning a surprise attack.

The sheriff considered what he needed to do. It was a three-day or more ride up the Animas Canyon to Boulder Gulch. But a single rider on a fast horse could get there in a little over two days by riding up through Stony Pass, which peaked at a breathtaking—quite literally—twelve thousand feet. He would take the treacherous path over the Rockies and warn Chief Ouray and his tribe of the impending danger. And if possible, he would try to ascertain if the rumors that Will Romney was among the tribe were true, whether against his will or otherwise.

He made the traverse in under two days. His horse proved all he could hope for, climbing the steep incline of the narrow pass flawlessly, plowing through the waist-deep snow near the peak, and agilely navigating the descent into the Ute camp. Approaching the encampment under a flag of peace, Otto was brought to Chief Ouray and told him about the Strickland militia on its way. The chief summoned Will to his lodge. Will explained to the sheriff that he was there voluntarily and didn't need rescuing.

"Well, son," the sheriff explained, "I don't think it matters to the Stricklands. I think this is all just an excuse to kill Indians." And as he said that, he looked ominously at Chief Ouray.

So, the three devised a plan.

The next morning as the sun rose, the Stricklands' militia assembled in an uneven line across an open field about a hundred yards from the Ute camp. To them, all appeared quiet, and some were downright gleeful in their expectation that the villagers were sleeping ducks just waiting to be shot in their beds. Little did they know that every warrior was awake and armed, ready for a surprise attack on the surprise attackers.

Then suddenly, Vanderhorn and Will Romney shocked them all as they rode out together to meet the militia.

"Goddamn Vanderhorn," muttered Jake. "That man needs killing."

"Gentlemen," the sheriff said to the Durangoans, "this here is Will Romney. He is here to tell you that he is with the Utes of his own accord, and he don't need no rescuing."

"That's right," Will said. "Been here near on to five years and they are like family to me. You all need to go home, and thanks for looking out for me."

"Liar!" Jake yelled. All three brothers were hotheads, but Jake was the hottest. Clearly Will's words had shocked the militia and removed any justification for this mission. Jake could feel his plan crashing. They had come so close to all that imagined gold and now it was slipping away.

"These savages done something to his brain!" Jake stammered. "Got him all twisted up in lies about his sorry self!" Jake then pleaded desperately, "If anyone needs rescuing, it's him! Think of his poor ma. We can't all just go back home and tell her we left him here!"

With that, Jake drew his gun and started the last fight of his life. He squeezed off a shot in the direction where Will sat in his saddle about twenty feet away. But Will was warrior-quick and in one deft motion, he slipped down behind his horse's head to avoid the incoming bullet, then swept like an acrobat under the horse's neck with a Colt 45 in hand. His single return volley, fired from beneath the horse's head, caught Jake Strickland square in the upper left chest, killing him instantly.

The other Strickland boys started for their guns, but Vanderhorn had them covered, and at that moment the Ute warriors leapt from their lodges and formed a line to confront the militia. For a moment all was silent. Then, strangely enough, of all people, Curly Johnston—who was bald as a billiard ball, and was never much of an influential personage back in Durango—rode out in front of the confused militia, turned his horse to face them, and said, "I don't know about you boys, but I ain't getting killed rescuing a boy that don't need nor want to be rescued!" Johnston abruptly spurred his horse and started back to town. One by one the Durango contingent joined him in a slow, meandering line, leaving only Caleb, Josh, and their dead brother facing Otto, Will, and Chief Ouray too, who had ridden out from the encampment to join them.

"I'm going to kill you if it's the last thing I do," Caleb hissed at Otto Vanderhorn, while Josh clumsily draped their dead brother over the saddle of his horse and secured it there with a lariat. Finally, they rode off.

In the end, however, the whole adventure got Will Romney thinking how he'd done his family wrong. Reluctantly but dutifully, he decided to accompany the sheriff back to Durango, and from there he continued on to Utah, hoping to reunite with his family. When he got to the old homestead, he found it inhabited by a new family. He learned that his mom had died, some said of heartbreak at losing her son to the savages. The nightmares of her son being cut and burned and beaten simply broke her mind, and her spirit, too. Three of his siblings had also died of disease and malnutrition. His father had given up the homestead and joined a band of Latter-day Saints who happened to pass through, and he continued on with them to Salt Lake City, where word was he found work as a schoolteacher.

Ashamed, Will ceased to look any further for his family. He became an army scout, then a Pony Express rider and a rodeo star. Eventually he settled in Jackson, Wyoming, where he married and went into politics.

Caleb Strickland was true to his word. The mythology of the West suggests that revenge was settled in certain ways. When one thinks of an "hombre" with a score to settle in the Old West, one imagines that hombre calling out his adversary for a brave and glorious shootout on Main Street at high noon. Or maybe he hires a faster gun to do his bidding and settle the score, like Jack Palance coming for Alan Ladd in the movie *Shane*. But that would take a real man or at least half a real man. But Caleb Strickland was a chickenshit. One day, soon after the battle of Boulder Gulch that never happened, he climbed up on the roof of the hotel on Main Street near the railroad and waited for Otto Vanderhorn. As the sheriff walked by below, Caleb shot him in the back of the head, nearly blowing the whole thing off his shoulders. Otto Vanderhorn was dead when he hit the ground. The town was so infuriated, vigilantes ran down Caleb before he could get away. They hung him from a tree in front of the Oar House. That tree is known as the hanging tree, and is still there today.

Chief Ouray and his people were eventually moved out of Boulder Gulch when the US government reneged on yet another treaty with this trusting chief, who only wanted peace and to coexist.

About ten years later, when the Utes were gone, a miner named Baker discovered one of the largest gold strikes in the history of Colorado in Boulder Gulch. It is estimated that the mine yielded over 20 million dollars' worth of gold and made Baker one of the richest men in Colorado.

12

TWILIGHT

As had become his habit, Zane Vanderhorn entered his barn and put his favorite saddle on Sage, a sorrel quarter horse that had become his daily companion for his twilight rides. So accustomed were they both to the routine that Zane barely needed reins, as Sage had the trail memorized. Their daily route took them north and west from the barn toward the red rock cliffs that Zane loved so much. About two hundred yards up the trail, there was a rise overlooking a bend in the river. From the top of that twenty-foot rise, he paused to gaze north with an unimpeded view of the valley. At this spot on a quiet night, a soft symphony could be heard as the water surged over the smooth rocks, banging them together in a sweet natural melody.

As was his custom, he slowly swung his arthritic hips out of the saddle and dismounted from Sage, and quietly knelt down on one knee in front of the two headstones. Charlotte, the love of his life, had blessed him with three sons, Otto, Witt, and Peter, as well as identical twin daughters, Elizabeth and Victoria. He had buried Charlotte and Victoria on this rise with the beautiful view near the singing water, after both had died from the cholera that had swept down from the mining towns. The other twin had miraculously survived. Elizabeth had grown to be smart, beautiful, and charming like her mother. Victoria died at nine, never having known a first kiss, a wedding day, or motherhood. There was no particular reason one lived and one died, just chance and luck. Such was life in the West.

He still couldn't believe that he had been alone for over twenty years. As his seventy-sixth year drew to a close, the loneliness grew harder every day. He had the satisfaction of a sprawling enterprise with various business interests all over the valley and beyond. The general store and stable had provided enough profits to buy and build the ZVH ranch. He built a beautiful hotel across from the railroad, as impressive as any in Denver, which catered to a new type of guests called tourists. The railroads, of which he was now a shareholder, made the valley accessible to an ever-increasing number of visitors, and there was money to be made in helping them enjoy their nostalgic visit to the Old West before it was gone. He had recently learned from a visiting engineer guest from the Rockefeller company that there were good prospects for oil in the area, and he had invested in this new industry.

The ranch was a classic, and well maintained, but not a huge going concern as far as cattle ranches go. Vanderhorn ran about two hundred head of cattle, "to keep in touch with the cowboy spirit," he used to say. He had about a thousand acres south of town, stretching between the regions where the South Mesa battle was fought and where, one day, a modern airport would be built. It was a good life, one that he would have loved to share with someone special, but it wasn't to be. Colorado was still far short on the female population at this point in time. Without doubt, Zane Vanderhorn, wealthy rancher and businessman, not to mention handsome and kind, was the most eligible widower in that part of the country. But nothing could help him forget his deceased wife, Charlotte, who was half of every good thing in his life from the moment he set eyes on her.

There was, however, one time when a woman did catch his eye. When he had a chance encounter in town with Lupita Chavez, he was immediately attracted to her, as if in some primal way her brokenness attracted his, even though he knew nothing of her past. He struggled through his conflicted emotions to let his interest in her be known. But Lupita Chavez's heart was completely closed to the idea of romance. The heartbreak over her disappeared Pedro Flores left no chance for the seeds of romance to find fertile soil in her heart ever again, even for this prosperous gringo.

Despite everything else, Zane took great satisfaction that his surviving children had built on the legacy he had created in the decades since he arrived in the valley with all his possessions stuffed in two saddlebags. Otto had served directly under U.S. Grant, the Civil War hero and president. Witt took over the family businesses and prospered in all he did. Ironically, he married Amorosa Chavez, the daughter of the woman who had so demurely rejected Zane. Peter went to university back East, the first Colorado-born individual to graduate from Harvard. He had returned to Durango and founded its first newspaper, *The Durango Tribune*. Elizabeth, the surviving twin, had attracted the attention of a fine young man, Ian McCallister, whose family was in railroads. After they married, she and her husband moved to Denver, where she participated in society circles, raised her three children, and did her best to influence the rich and powerful in ways that would benefit Colorado in the coming years. Yet two of her sons, Augustus and Woodrow, showed no interest in city life, and upon completing their education, they came back to Durango to live with Zane and to immerse themselves in the rugged Western life. As Woodrow once told his grandfather, "Life here in Durango is the real deal, like nowhere else on earth."

As Zane got back on Sage and followed the trail at the foot of the red cliffs, his heart was filled with gratitude for how good it had all turned out, far better than he ever could have expected upon his chance arrival in this Eden in the Rockies a half century earlier.

Farther on up the trail, he dismounted again, and he sat on a carved tree stump he had fashioned as a seat just for times like this. The sun was setting over the San Juans to the west. A gentle cool breeze touched his face, reminding him that the season was in the process of changing, and winter would soon return like an old and trusted friend. Shortly, the frigid winds would blow and the sunlight would prism through the snowcapped mountains at sunset, giving the optics of a crimson outline to the fourteen-thousand-foot peaks to the west as the day drew to an end. As day turned into night, glorious fluorescent colors filled the sky like a super-slow-motion fireworks display, first yellow, then orange, then red, then purple. And while fireworks colors dissipate in a flash, in this autumn sky, each color seemed to linger for eternity. When darkness overtook the colors, a canopy of a billion stars lit the sky as they have done for a billion years.

By God, this is beautiful, Zane thought. Though he had never thought much about the hereafter before, he mused that this must be what sunsets in heaven look like. His heart swelled in his chest, and he was at peace like no previous time in his life. "I wish Charlotte was here to see this," he said out loud. He smiled, leaned back in his tree chair, and took his last breath.

13

THE RANSOM

Sean McClintock felt lucky to be alive. After his parents died, and now saddled with trying to maintain and run their small farm, he had left his sister, Charlotte, at the homestead and headed to Ridgway for supplies. Disoriented and lost in the vast mountains and wilderness, he wandered to the brink of exhaustion and starvation. He only survived because the Steed family happened upon his nearly dead body as they passed through on their way to join the Brigham Young Mormons in the valley of the Salt Lake. Delirious and near death, Sean remained unconscious for his first two weeks with the Steeds, and for a few more weeks thereafter he was too weak to be much good for anything. Slowly, they nursed him back to health.

The Steeds were a good family, and they treated Sean well. Second cousins to Brigham Young, they were prosperous and well connected. They settled into a combination farm and ranch just outside town. In the two years after their arrival, they'd made a good start for themselves. Martin Steed was a devout Mormon, a solid citizen, and seemed to always prosper. His three wives, Bonnie, Naomi, and Ruth, had borne him six boys and six girls. Far from resenting Sean as an interloper, the Steed children welcomed Sean with the open arms of Christian charity. Though not considered family, they treated him as though he was. Martin Steed took Sean on as a hired hand and paid him generously for his contribution to the success of the family enterprise.

Sean showed his gratitude at every opportunity. He worked hard and lived thriftily, saving every penny he could so he could provision himself for the journey back to Colorado to see what had become of his sister. In due course, he saved enough money for a horse and pack mule, as well as a rifle and traveling supplies. With the full support of the Steeds, he planned to depart on the long journey back home.

On the day before his departure, a small, aggressive band of Chiricahua Apache arrived at the Steed homestead. The band of six was led by Scar, one of the fiercest of the Apache. They had come to trade. Ordinarily, trading with the Apache was a common part of life in Utah at the time. Desired goods were exchanged and acquired, and relationships were built. Most times, trading was good for everyone. But this day was different. Scar had come to sell two white sisters, ages eight and twelve, whom the Apache had abducted from their family in New Mexico. When Scar's intentions were made clear, Martin Steed adamantly refused to buy the girls, as human trafficking was strictly forbidden in his church.

Infuriated by the lack of cooperation, Scar threw the younger girl onto the ground and, with stunning ferocity, bashed her brains out with the butt of his rifle.

"You have no heart to let her die," Scar challenged. Pointing to the remaining girl, who trembled in fear, Scar yelled, "You let other one die too?"

Martin Steed froze, torn between his beliefs and the life of the surviving girl. Child stealing and slave trading were common among the tribes in the Southwest, but abhorrent to the Mormons. To Steed, buying a human being was unthinkable. He had not anticipated the brutality his refusal would trigger. Scar was not a patient man and he had no reservations about killing the remaining girl; that was clear. Angry at Steed's lack of response, he grabbed the girl and threw her on the ground next to her dead sister, mashing her face into a puddle of blood and brains. His murderous rampage stopped when a voice rang out, "I'll trade! I'll buy the girl!"

All eyes turned to Sean. He signaled to Scar to wait. Curious, Scar relented to see what this boy was up to. Sean ran to the barn and quickly returned. He led his horse and pack mule, loaded with all the supplies he had collected for his return trip to Colorado. He approached Scar and handed him the reins. From his saddle he retrieved his rifle and handed it to Scar. In one motion he reached down and picked up the trembling girl and backed away. Scar quickly inspected the rifle and the animals. Satisfied that he had made a good trade, he mounted his horse, handed the reins of his acquisitions to one of his six men, sneered at Martin Steed, and rode away.

That is how seventeen-year-old Sean McClintock came to own twelve-year-old Sarah Jordan.

To his way of thinking, Sean hadn't actually bought Sarah; he had bought her freedom. Sarah had only been with Scar for two months, but she was badly traumatized. When she was stolen, she had witnessed the killing and scalping of her parents and her brothers. Then she had seen her sister killed before her eyes as well. Only God knew what had happened to her over those two months in captivity, as Sarah refused to speak a word about her ordeal. Fortunately, she had not yet reached puberty and was more child than woman. Scar's tribe was particular about female captives: There was no limit on rape, mutilation, and humiliation of adult women, but girls were not to be touched sexually. Girls were strictly for trading, and unspoiled girls would bring a better price.

Sarah Jordan had suffered for one obvious treachery. One day she impulsively attempted to run away from her captors. Far from anywhere, with no plan or provisions, this running girl was swiftly caught by a young brave on horseback, who picked her up by the hair and dragged her to Scar. To discourage her from trying to run again, Scar smashed her right foot with his rifle butt, breaking numerous bones and disfiguring the foot, making it almost impossible for her to run, or even to walk normally.

The Steed family took pity on poor orphaned and crippled Sarah. Just like they had done with Sean, they took her into their bosom, not equal to family but special and valued. In a loving and nurturing environment, Sarah began to heal and slowly put her tragedy behind her.

She didn't talk much. She was obedient and compliant, a hard worker. She was extraordinarily grateful for having been rescued and given a chance at a new life. The realization that she was safe slowly filled her mind and consoled her spirit, such that over time, the nightmares about Scar became less and less frequent. But while she was so thankful for the Steeds, she never forgot that it was Sean who had saved her life. She watched him work around the place and noted his routine. She would find excuses to be where she knew he would be, yet when they were together, such as it was, she never tried to talk to him, as she hardly spoke to anyone. She would simply smile at the brave and handsome boy who had given so much to save her life.

With all his earthly possessions depleted in the ransom, Sean redoubled his efforts to provision himself all over again for a return to Colorado to search for his sister, Charlotte. Weeks of working and saving stretched into years. The Steeds were supportive of his efforts, but a long drought and a weak economy caused them all to suffer financially, also delaying Sean's departure. During those three years, Sarah entered womanhood. Despite her heavy limp, her natural beauty began to capture twenty-year-old Sean's attention in a different way. No longer the cute little shadow she had once been, Sarah was blossoming before his eyes. Over time, her hesitancy to talk began to fade, and she would make small talk with Sean now and then. One time she snuck a hot biscuit with honey from the kitchen and brought it to Sean as he worked in the barn. She handed it to him awkwardly and smiled, looking directly into his eyes, and remembering that this magic moment was only possible because of the ransom he had paid.

Sarah held a special place in Sean's heart, too. What started out as a big brotherly type of caring grew into true romantic feelings. In many ways, Sarah reminded him of Charlotte, and he felt the constant tug-of-war between staying in Utah with Sarah and finding his sister, wherever she might be in the Animas Valley.

The Steeds noticed and tacitly approved, almost in the way of cautious parents, of the budding romance between their two guests. Unfortunately, they were not the only ones who noticed.

Thelma was the daughter of an Indian whore and an unknown cowboy. Her mother had used both alcohol and laudanum during her pregnancy, causing Thelma severe developmental problems, as well as physical evidence of the fetal abuse. In short, Thelma was not pretty. Always a struggling outcast, Thelma was given a job by the good-hearted Steeds, who hired her to do cleaning, laundry, and other light household chores. Thelma talked regularly with Sean. He was kind and patient with her, something she rarely experienced, especially from men. In her desperate heart, she conjured the idea that Sean loved her and they would marry someday. When Sean talked about returning to Colorado, Thelma imagined herself accompanying him, leaving this lonely place and finding a new life with her lover, where she would be accepted. She dreamed of a home of her own, and children, too. Sean would rescue her just like he had rescued that little bitch Sarah Jordan, who forever seemed to be getting in the way. Nonetheless, she thought of her future with Sean every day.

Sean, however, never thought about her at all.

Everyone at the Steed homestead was aware of Sean's progress in readying himself for his trip to Colorado. Both Sarah and

Thelma paid particular attention, for different reasons, trying to estimate the days until he would actually leave. Sarah never imagined Sean's plan was for her to join him in Colorado. Thelma couldn't imagine that she wasn't going with him. These misunderstandings proved deadly.

One night at twilight, Sarah snuck into the barn to rendezvous with Sean. Her face was somber and she had been crying.

"What's wrong?" he asked.

"I heard the Steeds talking that you're leaving soon. I don't want you to go!" she cried. "I don't want you leaving me!"

"I ain't leaving you," Sean replied. "I need to go find my sister and get settled with a place for us. Once I take care of all that, I surely would like to come back for ya."

Sarah jumped into his arms, wrapping her small body around his, locking her legs around his hips. "You mean to marry me?"

"Yes, if you'll have me," Sean exclaimed.

"Of course!" Sarah answered. They kissed for the first time, both wishing the moment would last forever.

They were unaware that Thelma had stealthily followed Sarah into the barn and hidden in the tack room, a position from which she heard every word of their conversation. Infuriated that reality was injecting itself into her imaginary future, she devised a plan to get things back on track.

The next day Sean left for a far-off pasture to fix a fence. Thelma hatched her nefarious plan. Making sure no one was around, she approached Sarah as she was returning from the outhouse.

"Sarah, come quick, Sean's hurt!" she shouted. "In the barn, he got kicked in the head by a horse!"

Sarah ran into the trap. Thelma led her to a back stall. As Sarah entered in front of her, Thelma threw a rope around Sarah's neck and choked the life out of her. She dragged her body out the back door of the barn. About twenty yards away, in a slight dip, she buried Sarah in a shallow grave. Satisfied with her work, she returned to her business and, in her convoluted and delusional mind, back into the center of Sean's plans.

As evening approached, Sean returned from the fields. The Steeds took their usual places for mealtime. It soon became apparent that Sarah was missing. At first, they supposed that she might just be tardy, but as darkness fell, they became alarmed. The entire family and all the workers, as well as neighbors, scoured the grounds for signs of her whereabouts. As fearsome as the thought was, abduction crossed everyone's minds. Torches were lit by the dozens, Sarah's name being called endlessly. In a while, Brother James arrived with his tracking dogs.

Thelma panicked. Surely those dogs would find the grave! She needed to move the body! While everyone huddled to organize the search, Thelma bolted out the back of the barn and ran directly to the grave. She needed to get the dead girl out of the grave and drop her down the well where she would never be found. Then she would have Sean and Colorado and a home!

As Thelma was distracted with digging, she didn't hear Adam Steed, the eldest son, approach. In a burst, he lit his torch just as Thelma's digging revealed Sarah's muddied face. He screamed in horror. The whole search party came running, including Sean, who stared at the lifeless body of his murdered betrothed. In a panic, Thelma pulled a knife from under her skirt and began to wave it around, desperately trying to keep the men at bay. She became dizzy as she spun, until Adam Steed clubbed her skull with the butt of his rifle, knocking her to the ground. She was quickly subdued, hog-tied, and dragged to the barn, where she stayed under armed guard overnight.

The next day at the Steed homestead was both solemn and eventful. First, Sarah Jordan was buried in the family plot with a full entourage of mourners in attendance. Immediately thereafter, a quick trial was held, where Thelma was found guilty of the murder of Sarah Jordan and hung by the neck until dead from a rafter in the barn.

Heartbroken for Sean, the Steeds provided the balance of what he needed to begin his trip to Colorado to find his sister. With any luck, the four-hundred-mile trip could be accomplished in ten days. During that lonely saddle time, his mind drifted back to thoughts of Sarah and forward to thoughts of Charlotte. All these years he had wondered about her, unaware of her rescue, or her marriage to Zane Vanderhorn, or her role in the most prominent family in southwest Colorado. And he would never know that his sister had birthed a brood of children who started an empire that shaped Colorado for a hundred years.

Because Sean never made it. His trail ended a hundred miles short of his destination. With his mind distracted by his broken heart, he paid too little attention to his horse and the trail. With Sean's mind elsewhere, his horse caught a foot in a prairie dog hole, snapping its front right leg in two places, hurling Sean crashing onto a flat rock and breaking his neck. He died instantly in the middle of nowhere, halfway between his broken past and his unfulfilled dreams.

Days later, his body was found by a small group of starving, wandering old Apache. They stripped the clothing from his corpse, collected all of his belongings, and cooked and ate the rotting meat from his horse's carcass. It was the best meal they had had in months.

14

FREEDOM OF THE PRESS

Peter Vanderhorn was an idealist. His Ivy League education had given him an enlightened view of the nature of man. He was educated in the classics, philosophy, law, and government. He believed that mankind was on an upward progression of knowledge and civility. Perhaps those ideas played well in the classrooms in Cambridge, Massachusetts, but he would come to find out they didn't exactly translate to southwest Colorado in the final decades of the nineteenth century.

Peter loved his family ranch and legacy, but his real passion was being an instrument of change. He hated injustice and evil. His heart burned with a desire to make a difference, to somehow use his education and influence at every opportunity to leave the world better than how he found it. While living in Boston, he saw firsthand the power and influence newspapers had over the events of the day, how they could shape public opinion and even influence political discourse. He saw this as a blessing in the hands of a person of high ideals and solid character such as himself.

Upon returning to Durango and with his father's approval, Peter Vanderhorn launched The *Durango Tribune*, the first newspaper in the town. His news pages kept his readers up on all the events in the area, while his editorial pages were a venue for him to challenge the numerous injustices he saw, which so many others appeared to view as a normal and acceptable part of life in the West. Child labor, mistreatment of Native Americans and other minorities, miners' labor rights, excessive liquor and gambling, and prostitution were among the many targets of his progressive passions. But above all, Peter Vanderhorn was a crusader against criminal activity of any kind. He loathed those who preyed on the weak and powerless, who used violence against their fellow citizens with no conscience or regret. The *Tribune* was filled daily with specific details of crimes committed and the names of suspected perpetrators, as well as investigative reports of the "criminal cancer that infects Durango," as he called it. Not surprisingly, many of the reports of the crimes in the valley led directly or indirectly to the Stricklands.

Peter saw himself as a courageous crusader for good. He felt that right makes might. He had no fear of retaliation from the Stricklands because he was under the delusion that he was protected by the truth and justice he was advocating. He believed this was why he had not been threatened or molested by the Stricklands, or anyone of their ilk, for the stances he was taking.

After having spent four years in Boston, with its Eastern influences, Peter Vanderhorn was no longer solely of the West in thought. But he was surrounded by people who were all pure West, and in that gap was a potentially mortal risk for him. The criminal element in Durango didn't leave him alone out of respect or admiration. They were afraid to go after him for the pure and simple reason that his brother, Sheriff Otto Vanderhorn, was hell on wheels with a rifle or pistol. Otto could outfight, outrun, outhunt, and outshoot any man or woman in Colorado, and to harm his brother would most likely be a death sentence to the perpetrators.

Unrealized by Peter, this wall of protection disappeared when his brother was murdered by Caleb Strickland. The new sheriff, Roy Gentry, was the antithesis of his predecessor. His style, if one could call it a style, was much more of a hands-off, passive approach that overlooked many crimes and struck fear in the hearts of no one. Yet Peter continued his aggressive reporting, openly confronting the criminal element with a fervor, unaware that with each edition, he was going further and further out on a limb from which there was no turning back.

Then the powder keg blew. At the late end of one of his twelve-hour workdays, Peter slipped off into a nap around midnight. No one knows for sure whether the three masked men who entered by the back door knew he was there or were as surprised as he was. But break in they did, and they commenced mayhem on the offices of the *Durango Tribune* and its publisher. When Peter groggily rose from his chair, he was met with a blow of a pistol barrel across his forehead. Falling back into the chair, unconscious, he suffered three more blows, which opened a gash in his forehead and sent blood gushing out his broken nose.

Next, the three intruders turned to the printing equipment.

They scattered block print around the office and used crowbars to destroy the printing press. They flung files about, overturned desks, and poured buckets of ink around the office and over the next day's edition. The intruders raged at the *Tribune* and all it stood for. Peter came to and wiped blood from his face in shock. The leader of the vandals approached him.

"Stick to writin' about church socials if you know what's good for you," he mocked, before he again knocked Peter unconscious with a roundhouse blow of his right fist. As a humiliating exclamation point, he poured a can of ink over the defenseless man's bloodied head.

"That'll teach him," said Josh Strickland when he heard the news. "He don't have his hero brother around to protect him no more. The sheriff won't do a lick about this. It's just the newspaper man on his lonesome, and if he don't stop messin' in other people's business, he'll get worse than this."

As Strickland predicted, and Vanderhorn quickly learned, the sheriff would be of no help to him. "Sorry for your trouble, Vanderhorn," he said. "But with no description of the attackers to go on, there just ain't much I can do for you."

It appeared to Josh Strickland that Peter's idealism and passive nature, absent Otto's protection, left him vulnerable to continued abuse and intimidation. That same realization brought a smile to Strickland's face. He relished having a Vanderhorn to torment without fear of reprisal. But his enjoyment of the situation was short-lived.

No one knew what to make of Gus and Woodrow McAllister. They were the sons of Elizabeth Vanderhorn, who had married Ian McAllister of the railroad family and a prominent member of Denver society. Now in their early twenties, they had returned to Durango to live on the family ranch, forgoing city life as it were. The few times they ventured into town they were noted to be reserved and polite, quiet almost to a fault. From observation, to the ranchers and farmers and tradespeople used to working with their hands and often under harsh conditions outdoors, they appeared to be city soft. Such was the opinion of Josh Strickland when he set his men on their uncle.

There were no direct clues tying anyone to the attack on Peter Vanderhorn. But when anything like this happened in Durango, there was a suspicion that the Stricklands were somehow involved. At first there were no specific suspects to speak of. But over time, rumors, bragging, drunken conversation, and pillow talk with whores brought a picture into focus. Pretty soon, friends of the Vanderhorns passed the rumors along to the family. Whitey Maxwell and his two pardners, Big Head Mason and Gimpy Shruggs, had gladly done the hatchet job on the *Tribune*. Now and then in the employ of Josh Strickland when needed, they usually holed up in a small ramshackle cabin just south of the town of Purgatory.

Stone-faced, Gus and Woodrow checked their weapons and supplies, which included, oddly, an axe handle with no blade. They saddled their horses, then solemnly and without a word, they turned their horses north out of the ZVH toward Purgatory.

Two days later, the McAllister boys slowly rode their horses up Main Street toward the Broken Mustang. Josh Strickland was sitting in a chair on the porch outside the saloon's door, overlooking the goings-on in what he increasingly perceived to be his fiefdom in the absence of former sheriff Otto. Trailing behind the McAllisters were three horses with the ravaged bodies of Maxwell and his pardners hog-tied over their own saddles—not dead, but moaning in agony from some serious injuries. Their broken bones and bruises were too numerous to detail, but suffice it to say they involved noses, cheeks, skulls, and limbs, possibly a few other places. Whitey Maxwell's entire head was covered in ink. Gus and Woodrow came to a stop in front of Strickland, and Woodrow dropped the reins of the packhorses to the ground. Gus cut the three men loose, each hitting the ground face-first with a loud thump and a groan. Woodrow sat up erect in his saddle, pulled his duster jacket clear of his holster, and flipped off the leather strap, making sure Strickland could see this action.

"Strickland!" he bellowed for all to hear. "The freedom of the press will not be infringed upon!"

Woodrow glared directly into his enemy's eyes until Josh broke eye contact. Gus took one slow circle on his horse to look the gawking townsfolk in the eyes to make sure they got the meaning of the moment. Then, with a slight tug on the brim of his hat and a wry smile, he joined his brother as they rode slowly out of town.

The *Tribune* office was quickly repaired, the printing press was replaced, and the first real newspaper in Durango continues to be published to this day without any further interruption.

15

NIGHT RAIDERS

Hatred comes in many forms. Sometimes it is based on race, or nationality, or personal animosity. The hate that arose as the 1870s drew to a close in the valley was religious in nature.

Jedediah Jeffries arrived in Durango one spring and purchased a small patch of land along the river north of town, near the hot springs. His clan was notable for the large ratio of females to males. Jedediah, seventy with long gray hair and beard, was a distant cousin of Joseph Smith. His wife Ann was a woman of about fifty who was devout in all the teachings of the church, especially modesty.

Jedediah was a Mormon, of the Church of Latter-day Saints. As a follower of Joseph Smith, he ascribed to a theology that included traditional Christian beliefs, but also believed in Smith's teachings that began in Palmyra, New York, in the 1840s. One belief was that the history of North America was intertwined with the story of Israel and Jesus Christ, including the notion that Christ lived among

Native Americans after His crucifixion. Another was the practice of polygamy, which caused endless trouble for the Mormons everywhere. That is where Mormon trouble started in Durango.

Jedidiah Jeffries had a second wife named Hannah, who at thirty-five was half his age, as well as a third wife, Sariah, who was close to forty. The brood included three sons—Joseph and Mitt, in their thirties, and Ammon in his twenties—as well as three daughters—Prudence in her late twenties, Madelyn, early twenties, and Ashtyn, not quite twenty. Or so it appeared to the people of Durango.

In any case, the arrival of the Jeffries clan in the valley created quite a reaction from the townsfolk across the board. The church folk were appalled at the intrusion of what they saw as a corrupt religion into their community. The saloon crowd resented an old coot like Jeffries hogging so many women. Why should he have three wives when most men didn't even have one? In those days, men still outnumbered women five to one in Colorado. It just didn't seem fair! And he had those three daughters, too, and no man was allowed near them.

It didn't take long for this precarious situation to come to the attention of Josh Strickland, the last remaining son of Bart and Slow Eyed Mary. The deaths of his father and two brothers had been a setback for Josh, both personally and professionally. Besides being alone now, he had always been a follower. He missed his father and brother's initiative to start new ventures, as well as their partnership in carrying out the schemes they thought up. After the death of Caleb and Jake, he had begun mentoring Caleb's two boys, Wade and Griff, in the ways of the family business. He enjoyed teaching these young teenagers the outlaw life, as well as sharing the family stories around a good campfire. They had not yet conducted any jobs together, but the time was coming. Not wanting to risk a big job like a bank or payroll robbery, Josh was looking for a small-time opportunity to see what they were made of. The Jeffries family seemed to be a prime target. They had money and means, and were not in a good position to defend themselves, what with all those women and all. Besides, the boys would be needing some women soon, and the Jeffries daughters, especially Ashtyn, were, collectively, as good a stable of prospects as any.

Ashtyn Jeffries had also caught the attention of Woodrow McAllister. He had seen her with her family when they were both procuring supplies at the Vanderhorn General Store. His attempt to introduce himself was blocked by Jedediah, who sensed the young man's intention and whisked her out of the store.

Woodrow knew the location of the Jeffries place, and he knew all the trails in the area, so he took every opportunity to ride near her property on the off chance that they might meet. Luck was with him one afternoon when he happened upon Ashtyn picking wildflowers in a meadow away from the main house.

Tipping his hat, he said, "Good day, miss. I would like to introduce myself. I am Woodrow McAllister."

"I know who you are, from the store," she replied with a warm, friendly smile. "Besides, everyone in Durango knows who you are." That began a conversation that lasted hours, filled with the awkward words, gestures, and sometimes silence that is the seed from which young love blossoms. That "chance" encounter led to many others, every chance they could, always in secret from her family.

"Jedediah would give me a beating if he found out about us," Ashtyn warned. Ever careful, they couldn't deny the attraction they felt for each other and didn't even try. After weeks of awkward courtship, Woodrow gazed into her eyes as they lay upon a blanket near the river. Having no experience to draw upon, he sensed that there was a kiss to be had. Nervously, he leaned in with lips at the ready, only to be met with a crash of her forehead into his mouth as she reached for a bite from their picnic. They both jumped in shock. Ashtyn giggled in embarrassment, then realized Woodrow's lip was bleeding. To make sure he didn't misinterpret the awkward collision as rejection, she wiped the blood from his lip, and then locked her lips on his in a way that changed his life.

Unfortunately, Woodrow McAllister wasn't the only visitor to the Jeffries place those days. Those nights, to be more accurate. Josh Strickland and his nephews, not quite ready for big-time crime, had made a habit of getting liquored up at the Broken Mustang and then riding out to harass the Mormons. The three didn't have any particular bone to pick with the Jeffries family. They didn't care a lick about their odd religion, religion itself being a foreign entity to the Stricklands altogether. But with a father over seventy and three soft sons, they looked like easy pickings. Josh's hunch proved to be true, as their nighttime forays that started with petty vandalism soon escalated to other random mischief like setting fires and firing random gunshots in the air. The lack of response from any Jeffries emboldened them even more, until Griff suggested, "Let's take one of the women."

The harassment of the Jeffries family didn't go unnoticed by the townspeople. Problem was, nobody seemed to care. Lots of people would be happy to see the Mormons run out of the valley. Sheriff Gentry was too lazy and beholden to the Stricklands to get involved. As the attacks escalated, Woodrow could sense the fear in Ashtyn during their rendezvous. So he decided that if no one else was going to step in to defend the family, then he would. He outfitted himself with provisions for an overnight watch from a spot on a hillside about a half mile from the Jeffries main house. Sitting with his back to a tree, wrapped in a blanket, he was dozing off when he heard the sound of gunshots. Startled to his feet, he saw the Jeffries barn ablaze and people running everywhere. After leaping onto his horse, he set out at a gallop, Winchester in hand. On a dead run, he let go his first shot at one of the three mounted riders, hitting him in the thigh. Closing in, he recognized a rider with a lasso in hand chasing down Ashtyn. Firing again, he gave that rider second thoughts about hurling that lasso. Woodrow reached the main house, firing away at the night raiders as the Jeffrieses scrambled for protection behind him. Foiled, Josh Strickland, Griff, and wounded Wade turned tail and ran for town.

With the attack over, the family turned their attention to the fire consuming the barn. Despite their efforts, the fire was too hot and the wind too strong. The barn was lost. To make matters even worse, embers from the barn flew to the house, and small fires there did considerable damage to the roof of the main house before they could be extinguished.

Jedediah Jeffries approached Woodrow warily and said, "I'm not sure why you came along when you did, but thank you for your help." Satisfied that Ashtyn was safe for the night, Woodrow returned to his camp on the hillside, where he continued his watch over the Jeffries homestead.

The next morning, Woodrow was awakened by Ashtyn approaching up the hill. As he stood to greet her, he saw over her shoulder, off in the distance, the rest of the Jeffries family packing their belongings into their wagons.

Tearfully, Ashtyn revealed, "We're pulling out. Heading for the Salt Lake. Jedediah doesn't want to fight the hate anymore."

Impulsively, Woodrow blurted, "Stay with me!"

"With all my heart I wish I could, but I can't," she replied. "Jedediah would never allow it."

"Why not?" Woodrow asked. "A father wants a good, upstanding husband for his daughter, doesn't he?"

Ashtyn trembled in fear and from the horror of what she was about to say. "I am not his daughter . . ." She burst into tears. "I am Jedediah's wife!"

Speechless, Woodrow took Ashtyn in his arms. Through sobs she told him of her arranged marriage at fourteen to a man who was fifty years her senior, of the loss of innocence, and of the loveless matrimony to a man old enough to be her grandfather.

When she had cried herself out, Woodrow lifted her up on his horse, setting her down sidesaddle. Then, placing his left foot into the stirrup, he swung himself onto the saddle behind her, and the two of them rode down the hill to the gathered Jeffries clan.

"Jeffries," Woodrow started, "I am here to tell you that I have asked Ashtyn to be my wife, and she has agreed." The shocked family stopped their packing.

Jedediah Jeffries angrily responded, "You can't marry her. She's already married to me!"

"Well," Woodrow answered, "if you can have more than one wife, I reckon she can have more than one husband." The stone-cold expression on his face made it clear that the matter was settled. Woodrow turned his horse and headed for the ZVH with his new fiancée riding double, his arms wrapped tightly around her as he held the reins. The Jeffries family left the valley the next day and never returned. Woodrow and Ashtyn were married the day after the Jeffrieses' departure, by a justice of the peace in the Durango Town Hall.

That's the story of how Ashtyn Jeffries became Ashtyn McAllister, and how Woodrow McAllister became the first and only bigamist in the Vanderhorn family. Because all of Durango believed Ashtyn to be Jedediah's daughter, their bigamy remained a secret never before divulged until the writing of this book.

16

THE RUNAWAY

Clara Watson knew she was in trouble and began to panic. At sixteen, Clara was nearly eight years younger than Wade Strickland. Young and innocent, she had fallen for his sweet talk and persistent attention hook, line, and sinker. When Wade asked her to run away with him, she jumped at the chance to leave the drudgery of pioneer life for the freedom and adventure on the road with a brave and charismatic older man she presumed was deeply and eternally in love with her. The time and date were set when Wade would whisk her away to a new life together.

Wade saw things a little differently. He saw Clara as an easy mark, and he enjoyed the thought of having himself a virgin for a change. He included her in his plans to head north, where he would have her alone and show her a few things before he dumped her somewhere on his way to Montana. He hadn't exactly figured that part out yet, but all in due course, he thought.

Wade didn't talk much on the trail. His gentle, charming persona quickly gave way to a harsh trail boss demeanor before Durango was even out of sight, as they headed for Silverton. They had hardly set up camp on the first night before Wade was on Clara. It was nothing like she imagined. There was no romance or tenderness, just hurt. Wade didn't seem to care how she felt. In fact, this innocent and inexperienced girl could tell he didn't care about her at all.

She had made a huge mistake.

With no one to help her and nowhere to go, Clara resigned herself to the abuse from Wade. When she tried to talk to him, he simply said, "Shut up, you little bitch!" She tried as best she could to control herself, but she couldn't hold back the tears of regret for being so gullible. Why had she been so stupid? As the tears rolled, she began to sob.

"If you don't quit your whining, I'm gonna throw you off this cliff!" was Wade's response. It was clear to Clara that he would do it, too.

Clara knew she needed to get away from Wade; she just didn't know how to do it. So, she waited through two more nights of assault and abuse before they arrived at their destination. Silverton was not the place for a young girl. It was populated with two kinds of people, whores and men looking for whores. The miners lived in desperate isolation, scraping by on the low wages gained through their hazardous work. They had no other options; mining was the only economic engine in the town. Brawls, shootings, and stabbings were commonplace occurrences, and women were as vulnerable to mayhem as men, maybe even more so. Clara was no safer here than with Wade on the trail.

Upon arrival in Silverton, Wade went directly to the Shady Lady and ordered dinner. As he wolfed down a plate of greasy bacon and boiled potatoes, he scowled at Clara and tossed her a biscuit. With that appetite taken care of, he arranged for the company of Sadie, a whore already well known to him. Heading up the stairs, he pushed Clara ahead of him, saying, "You sit and watch and see how it's supposed to be done."

Clara was horrified as she was forced to sit and watch this monster and whore go about their lustful business. Strickland was an animal. Sadie was no better. When they were done, Strickland almost immediately drifted off to sleep in a drunken stupor, while Sadie retreated to an overstuffed chair in a far corner of the room, counting her night's earnings, until she, too, began to doze off. This left Clara Watson to ponder her serious error of judgment, petrified about what had become of her life.

Clara awoke the next morning to the sound of Sadie using the chamber pot. It was just the two of them.

"Where's Wade?" Clara asked, as Sadie hoisted up her knickers.

"Off to Wyoming or Montana or wherever, I reckon," Sadie replied. She smiled a kind smile at Clara and consolingly laid a gentle hand on her shoulder. "You thought you was going with him, didn't you, sweetie?"

Astonished, Clara tried to determine whether being abandoned by Strickland was better or worse than being forced to stay with him. Now that she was released from that monster but deserted by him, she was stranded in a whorehouse in the middle of a tough mining town. The gnawing panic that had plagued her mind all the way from Durango now filled her soul.

Sadie looked at Clara with pure pity. She remembered her long-gone days of innocence, when her future held the promise of love and happiness and prosperity. Those were days she knew she had no chance to recover for herself, but feeling a soft sense of compassion that she had not felt in a long time, Sadie sensed that she might be able to help recover such prospects for Clara.

"Let's get you to the sheriff," Sadie said, much to Clara's relief.

Sheriff Clay Ogden rose up from his chair to meet the two women as they entered the jail. He grabbed a blanket from a cell and wrapped it around the shivering Clara. Observing that the new day wasn't that cold, the sheriff realized that Clara was shivering from sheer anxiety and fear.

"Wade Strickland left her here," Sadie said, exchanging knowing looks with the sheriff. Before she walked back out the door, Sadie looked at Clara and said, "Sheriff Clay will take care of you, darlin'."

Sheriff Ogden hustled up some breakfast for the starving girl. Gratefully, she ate her fill as she pondered her future. As Ogden questioned her, she revealed her story, omitting the lurid details. But Ogden knew Wade Strickland and didn't need to be told the rest.

"We need to get you back home," Ogden declared.

Luck would have it that Gus McAllister was in town, having helped his friend Ogden out by delivering an escaped prisoner. Reading the signs of the situation, Gus readily agreed to bring the girl home. Clara knew well of the McAllisters and Vanderhorns and couldn't believe her good fortune to be placed into his care and protection. She couldn't wait to get home and put this nightmare behind her.

The descent toward Durango went smoothly at first. Gus was a gentleman and treated Clara with respect and care. It appeared Clara's troubles would soon be over, until they reached the expansive green valley floor that stretched out just below where a ski resort is today. In the distance, blocking their path, rode a raiding party of five Indians. Unknown to Gus, Scar and his band of raiders had wandered to the north in search of new places to plunder. Gus didn't know exactly who this group was, but he knew he and Clara were in trouble. Quickly, they spurred their horses and sprinted to a large pile of driftwood beside the river. In one motion, Gus dismounted, grabbed his rifle and ammo, and forted up.

The attackers swiftly closed the distance. A bullet whizzed by Gus's head. He returned fire and killed the rider on the far left. Ducking for cover, he handed Clara one of his pistols with a stern look into her eyes to make sure she got the meaning. She did.

Of all the fears on the frontier, the biggest was becoming a captive. Every schoolgirl and boy had heard all the horrific stories of captives—mostly children and babies—who were found abused and mutilated. Over time the stories took on lives of their own, darker and more horrifying with each retelling. Cut-off arms, fingers, feet, and noses were rumored to be the common atrocities. Those fears were reinforced by the occasional return of a captive who had endured precisely this kind of mutilation. Every frontier child was raised with the understanding that captivity was a fate worse than death, and a calamity to be avoided even at the cost of death by one's own hand.

Clara knew what the gun was for.

That settled, Gus McAllister coolly went back to their defense. One Apache made a frontal charge at Gus, hooting and screaming in a display that was the mark of bravery to his peers. Gus honored his bravery with a Winchester blast that blew the attacker's face off. What followed was a two-hour standoff of long-range gunfire with no advantage gained by either party. Gus realized that time was not on their side, so he devised an audacious plan. Leaving Clara secure in the makeshift driftwood fort, he mounted his horse, rifle in hand, and began a full-gallop charge across the open field directly at the well-hidden attackers. Stunned and impressed, Scar rose to a standing position, aimed, and fired, knocking Gus out of his saddle as Clara looked on in horror. For what seemed like eternity, nobody moved. Then, Scar sent his two remaining fighters to check Gus's body and bring back his scalp. They would then go for the girl, who would make good trading when they were done with her.

Gus waited silently as the two attackers approached. He had tossed his rifle aside as he threw himself, unharmed, out of his saddle just as Scar's long-distance shot went wide. His gamble paid off. He heard the hooves of the attackers' horses as they approached, heard the two attackers laughing, casual and unaware as they dismounted. As they walked toward him, scalping knives in hand, he quietly cocked the hammers on the pistols he held in each hand, as he lay facedown. When he felt the hand reach for his hair, he spun in a burst and killed both men before they realized they had been duped. With an extra bullet to each to make sure they were dead, Gus grabbed his rifle and let loose a barrage toward the stunned Scar, who jumped on his horse and surrendered the field.

With the satisfaction of a job well done, Gus mounted his horse and returned to the driftwood fort. There, to his shock and dismay, he found Clara dead from a gunshot blast to the temple. His actions had been so fast and instinctive, the situation so dire in its potential consequence, that he'd had neither the time nor the means to somehow communicate to Clara his ingenious plan to play possum. The second Gus dropped from his horse and hit the ground, she assumed the worst and did what every frontier girl knew to do. She took her own life to avoid the savage captivity she wrongly assumed was her fate.

Horrified at the turn of events, Gus buried Clara in a marked grave in the soft black soil along the banks of the Animas River. Anticipating that the news of her needless death would bring shock to her parents, he decided not to compound their pain by delivering the body of their precious daughter with one side of her head blown off. He gathered the three ponies his adversaries had been riding and decided to give them to the Watsons as a small compensation for their loss.

As Gus rode the lonely remainder of the trail to Durango, he thought a lot about luck, or fate, or destiny. Just one small thing here, one other decision there, and Clara would still be alive. But it wasn't to be. In the West, that's just how it was. Today wasn't her day, Gus thought. It was just that simple.

It wasn't Clay Ogden's day, either. Only hours after Gus McAllister left on his mission of mercy to restore Clara to her family, the Wilkins gang arrived in Silverton, having broken some of their members out of jail in Telluride. Known as wanted men, they were confronted by Ogden and his shotgun outside the Shady

Lady. A fair fight it wasn't, six against one. Ogden was killed on the main street at midday, but not before killing two of the gang. As Ogden lay in the street, life draining from his veins, he looked for the last time at the snowcapped peaks and glimmering aspens that rimmed the valley, and thought there were worse places than this to die. And then he did.

Unknown to the Wilkins gang, Blaine Cragg, the local mine owner, fed up with crime in Silverton, had formed an informal vigilante committee, promising a day's wages to any citizens who would help him deal with the criminal element that dominated Silverton. Upon hearing the gunshots, the vigilantes were up in arms. Bill Wilkins escaped, but his three surviving accomplices were corralled by the vigilantes. Caught up in the emotion of the moment, the vigilantes beat and abused their captives as they led them to the Shady Lady, where all three bloodied bodies were hung by the neck from the second-floor balcony as a warning to the world that crime would not be tolerated in Silverton.

These were the last recorded lynchings in Silverton. The message was understood.

17

KISSIN' COUSINS

Nell McGuire was in a sweat, as she jumped into the horse-drawn carriage in front of the Strathmore Hotel near Trinity Church on Wall Street. As she ordered the driver uptown, she noticed a bloodstain on her dress and covered it with her shawl. This one had been hard. The previous nine men had been much easier. She thought she had her game plan perfected, but it turned out it still needed work.

Abruptly, everything had changed. She knew her time in New York was coming to an end and she needed a new scam, and quick. Bored at the slow pace of the ride, Nell opened the newspaper she had taken off the dead man in the hotel room. On page one of the *Herald Tribune* was the headline—

POLICE BELIEVE NINE MURDERS ARE THE WORK OF ONE WOMAN

LEADS ARE BEING FOLLOWED UP

Was it true or a ploy? Nell couldn't take a chance. But what could she do, and where could she go? Her mind blank, she thumbed through the pages of the newspaper until an ad for a book caught her eye. It was a dime-store novel called *The Colorado Kid*. Her mind raced. From way back in her memory she pulled out a nugget. One of her distant cousins on the Drummond side had gone out West, changed his name to Strickland, and was doing big things. She needed a lifeboat, and maybe the *Herald Tribune* had just sent it to her.

Two thousand miles away, Griff Strickland was in a pickle. He needed a woman in his life. The plan to kidnap Ashtyn Jeffries had blown up, thanks to the intervention of his nemesis, Woodrow McAllister. He was getting desperate and running out of options. For most cowboys, the local whores could fill the need, so to speak. But that wasn't working out for him on account of a small problem. Fact of the matter was, Griff was cursed with very small equipment. Not just below-average small, but *really* small. Whores laughed when they saw his tiny unit, and at times, Griff was mortified by his suspicion that they joked and giggled about it among themselves, behind his back. More than one laughed in his face on first glimpse, leading to a punch in the face from Griff. It happened enough times that he was banned from the brothel, even though it was a Strickland family owned and operated enterprise.

"Sorry, Griff," Uncle Josh Strickland had said with a sarcastic laugh. "You're gonna need to get your pokes elsewhere. You can't keep beating up my whores and putting them outta commission for a week at a time. Besides, it ain't the whores' fault you got a dinky pecker."

In Colorado at that time, except for the very few married men, there were two kinds of men: those who got theirs from whores and those who didn't get any at all. Sadly, Griff was resigning himself to a life of the latter. He couldn't know that a continent away a distant relative was launching a scheme that would change everything.

Nell McGuire wasn't a whore. She was an escort. Men didn't pick her; she picked them. Once she eyed a target, she would approach boldly, flatter incessantly, and seduce hotly. She was a Georgia peach, as the expression goes, a Southern belle with a disarming charm that would melt Yankee men's hearts like an Atlantic City boardwalk snow cone in July. She sought out men of means. No whorehouses for her. She insisted on being wined, dined, and bedded in the finest hotels in the city. Her company could be had for an appreciative gratuity, and on that alone she was living well. Then one day, an opportunity presented itself. Her mark, an old man named Peters, fell into a deep sleep after their romp. Bored, she decided to take her gratuity and leave the old buzzard snoring away. When she opened his billfold, she found it stuffed with cash, nearly five hundred dollars. Ten times what she would expect to be paid by him. As she was taking the money and stuffing it in her brassiere, old man Peters woke up.

"You little bitch!" he yelled. "I'll have you arrested!"

Nell believed he was bluffing, as he wouldn't want to have to explain to the police or his wife how he had come to be in the company of this woman who had stolen his money. But Nell couldn't be sure, and without thinking, she bashed his brains in with a lamp from the night table, then quietly made her escape.

Some women would find themselves crippled with guilt at the realization that they had just committed murder. Nell, on the other hand, found it exhilarating. She had never felt so alive as when she killed that old creep who, to her way of thinking, deserved it. This, Nell thought, would be her new plan. Love them to death, she thought with a laugh. But the plan soon came unwound, as her marks didn't fall asleep quite so accommodatingly as old man Peters had. And at a petite but shapely five feet tall and ninety-five pounds, she was much smaller than most of her targets. Overpowering her marks was out of the question. No, for her plan to work, she needed another advantage.

That edge came when she went to the dentist with a bad tooth.

"It needs to be pulled," Doc Richards stated matter-of-factly.

"I can't let you do it. It will hurt too much," Nell replied.

"Don't worry," the Doc said reassuringly. "I can put you to sleep through the whole procedure; you won't feel a thing." Smiling broadly, he showed her a bottle of chloroform like it was some kind of magic potion. Nell was intrigued.

He knocked her out good, pulled the tooth, and then left the room, allowing Nell ample time to come to. When he returned, he brushed her hand lightly with his, the way a parent might wake a sleeping child. "How are you?" he asked gently.

"I'm fine," she replied, feeling like she was awakening from the deepest sleep of her life, although the place where the bad tooth had been throbbed slightly with mild, but manageable pain.

"That stuff is wonderful," she remarked.

"Indeed it is," Doc Richards replied. "Makes some parts of my work a whole lot easier . . . for my patients, I mean."

"Doctor," Nell purred coyly, "do you think you could give me that bottle?"

"Oh, no!" he said, shaking his head. "This is very potent stuff. It's for medical purposes only."

But as he spoke, Nell gently ran the soft, well-practiced fingers of her right hand against his inner thigh. Doc Richards looked into her eyes and understood that a wordless negotiation was taking place. Lustily, he agreed to the trade. In return for a quick romp in his dentist chair, a beaming, almost giddy Nell McGuire left the office that afternoon carrying a full bottle of chloroform. She turned to look at Doc Richards as he rested in the chair that had been their temporary love nest. For a brief instant, Nell considered killing him, but she thought better of it, in case she might need a refill someday.

On her next date, Nell waited for Ira Goldbaum to drop his guard, watching as he lay naked on the bed, lolling off into a blissful sexual afterglow, his eyes rolling, then slowly closing as if to slumber. She quickly reached into her satchel, pulled out her chloroform-soaked handkerchief, and held it over his unsuspecting face until he fell limp. She located his clothing, draped over an ornate Queen Anne–style upholstered armchair, and looted his pants pockets and vest of cash, his pocket watch, and his jewelry. She paused, looking about the room with an air of satisfaction as she began to consider her exit. She looked at him lying motionless on the bed, helpless, as if dead, and she thought, "Why not?" And with that, she grabbed a steak knife from the room-service cart and plunged it into his heart with all her might.

Maybe I'm a little weird, she thought to herself, as the life poured out of Goldbaum's chest. *But I feel so alive when they're dying.*

And so began the reign of terror for the philanderers of New York City. Nell became a sultry Southern predator, like a shark who smells blood in the water. Ten horny adulterers met their demise in this dastardly way, with Nell becoming more exhilarated with each brutal murder. The more she killed, the more she wanted to kill again. And she was becoming rich in the process. But her time was running out. The recent headlines splashed sensationally across all of the New York newspapers of the day made it abundantly clear to Nell that a change of scenery was in order, and soon.

After a few family inquiries, she learned that her distant relatives had settled in the Animas Valley. As the police were closing in, she raced to deposit her stolen treasures in a safe deposit box at the Morgan Bank on Wall Street. With that accomplished, she headed west by rail out of the stately Grand Central station to Denver, proceeding from there by stagecoach to Durango.

Before leaving New York, she sent a telegram ahead to inform her erstwhile unknown family of her impending arrival. Somewhat perturbed that none of her so-called relatives showed up to greet her at the stage depot in Durango, she inquired of the clerk where she might find any Stricklands, and she was directed to the Broken Mustang. Her walk along the few blocks from the stage to the saloon was like a debutante at the ball. Every head turned as this well-dressed, well-heeled Southern belle with a parasol sauntered across town, past the mud puddles in the dirty streets. Nell made sure all eyes were on her, walking slowly in the manner, she imagined, of European royalty.

When she entered the Broken Mustang, everything stopped. Even the piano player stopped playing. You could hear a feather fly, it was so quiet. Faking embarrassment, Nell blushed and asked, "Can anyone tell me where I might find one of my long-lost family, the Strickland clan?"

Griff jumped to his feet and introduced himself, nervously rubbing his grubby hands on the front of his liquor- and tobacco-stained shirt. He escorted her to a table, where she proceeded to pour out the sad, concocted story of what brought her to the West. Orphaned at a young age, Nell claimed, she was subsequently raised by nuns who had recently put her out because she was "having lustful thoughts about men." Nell covered her mouth with one hand as she said this, as if she was ashamed of ever having such thoughts. As she continued to weave her story, Nell really poured it on with the embellished details and with the flirting—especially the flirting, occasionally glancing down to make sure her ample cleavage was showing nicely. And all along, an enraptured Griff Strickland swallowed her bait, hook, line, and sinker, washing it down with a half-dozen mugs of the saloon's rank-tasting beer on draft.

Nell got herself a room at the General Platt Hotel and proceeded to set her trap. Griff was an easy mark, she surmised immediately. He was an inexperienced, gullible lout whose brains, if he had any, had been dulled by years of unfulfilled lust, too much liquor, and perhaps also, Nell theorized, a kick in the head or two from a steer run amok. She showered him with teasing attention as the weeks passed, a soft touch of the hand here, a quick peck on the cheek there. One time while walking, she slid her hand down to his butt for just an instant. Griff thought he would die from that touch alone. Finally, he had the attention of a woman all to himself, and she was captivating, aggressive, and uninhibited. Gone were his rude, crude, violent ways with women that were so common among the men in his family. Nell was not a whore; she was the first real lady he had known—she had more class, Griff reasoned, than any other woman in the entire town—and she had him on the run.

Griff's big fear was that his smallness, once revealed, would end the romance. It caused him to hesitate about getting more physical. Nell couldn't understand his hesitation. That was not a response she had ever encountered before. Because she was seen in town as a lady, all upright and dignified, Nell never had occasion to be among the whores who might have casually filled her in on Griff's physical lacking. She would need to find out for herself.

Nell ran out of patience. One day she paid a young boy a nickel to take a note to Griff at the Broken Mustang, inviting him to join her in her room. He hurried over, and, upon entering, found Nell completely naked. Griff panicked! Soon she would know his size and the romance would end, he feared. Fortunately for him, Nell didn't respond negatively at all, and Griff gleefully jumped into this new affair. Their romps became nearly an everyday event. Griff had never been so happy or had his needs so cared for. This must be love, he thought.

One down, one to go, Nell thought. *This is going just like I planned.*

Griff was trapped like a coyote in a steel trap, but he had no intention of chewing his leg off to escape. Now it was time for part two of her devious plan.

Everyone called him Ox. No one knew his Christian name or surname. Just Ox. He worked a small claim north of town, where his size and bulk and sheer strength could be put to good use. Ox was strong, and he was also simple as a child. At first he just took Nell's attention as friendliness. But as she became more bold and more forward, he started to connect that she was interested in the things the whores do. Ox's brain didn't move fast or make connections easily, but Nell made her intentions hard to miss. That all became clear one night when she asked him to her room for some "help," and after a bit of coaching and explaining, their affair began. As she planned, Nell worked hard to keep this two-timing going at a fever pitch. For her plan to succeed, she needed both men to be head-over-heels foolishly in love with her, and for each to believe that they were the only one in her heart.

She played the two men like a pair of dueling player pianos. Hopelessly in lust or love or whatever, these hapless men were drawn further and further into her web.

Her original plan only involved one scam against Griff. That all changed when Ox brought her a gift. Sitting on her bed like a shy schoolboy, he reached out his enormous paw and held out a purse-sized bag.

"Take it," Ox said with a dumb grin.

It was heavy. Very heavy. She opened it and her eyes widened at the sight of the largest solid gold nugget she had ever seen.

"It's yours," Ox repeated, "because you're my girl and I love you. There's plenty more where that come from," he offered. He told Nell that he had some success on his claim that he "kept real quiet about." It turned out that Ox had about forty thousand dollars in gold hidden beneath the floorboards of the dilapidated cabin he had built on his claim. "I don't trust banks," he explained, chuckling as he said it. Ox's preferred fiduciary policy aside, Nell surmised that he wasn't quite as addle-brained as he might appear. This required a slight adjustment to her original plan.

Immediately, even as she was sitting there with Ox, Nell reformulated her exit plan. Her trap had two rats sniffing for the cheese, and the trap was about to snap.

"With that kind of money we can get married," she whispered. "Let's do it! We'll elope tomorrow!"

She made a plan for them to gather their belongings, including the gold of course, and meet at noon by the river just south of town. From there the pair would head for California and the good life.

The next morning, after her pre-breakfast romp with Griff, she said, "You know, Griff, I don't really trust banks. They're forever getting robbed and such. I sure would feel more secure about our future if we had that money where you could guard and protect it." She placed her hand on his inner thigh and smiled.

At Nell's direction, Griff dutifully went to the bank and drew out all his money, nearly fifteen thousand dollars. When she saw the currency-filled sack, she smiled wryly and said, "Let's go someplace and celebrate," and she directed him to the same spot where she would be meeting Ox. It was half past eleven when they arrived.

After some flirting and small talk, Nell laid herself out on the blanket and invited dumb, clueless Griff to romance. As she had hoped, it wasn't too long before Ox arrived. As soon as she saw him, she recoiled from Griff and began to scream at the top of her lungs, "Rape! Rape! Please help me!"

Griff was startled. Ox flew into a rage. He lifted half-naked Griff in the air and body-slammed him to the ground. Knocking the wind out of him, Ox sat on Griff's chest and with his two great paws choked the life out of him. So intense was his focus that he barely heard Nell approach him from behind, until she jumped on his back and reached around his head with both arms, pushing a chloroform-soaked kerchief over his face. Knowing his sheer bulk, Nell had used all of the chloroform left in the bottle, just to make sure it would be enough to knock him out. Ox toppled over unconscious, right next to Griff's dead body.

So thick were the muscles in Ox's chest that try as she might, Nell couldn't get her knife to penetrate for a lethal blow. And Ox was such a big man that the large dose of chloroform quickly began to wear off. In a panic, she grabbed Griff's pistol and shot Ox in the chest, point-blank. Then she rolled herself around in the dirt and bramble, inflicting numerous cuts and scrapes and tattering her dress. When she had made a sufficient mess of herself, she jumped on Griff's wagon and headed to town. But first she took Ox's gold from his saddlebag, combined it with Griff's cash, and sequestered it in the wagon. This was no mean feat for a petite girl like her; the stuff was heavy as hell, and she could barely lift the huge nugget Ox had given her. She rehearsed her story on the way to town. She and Griff were out for a picnic. Ox came along and, in a fury, attacked Griff and tried to rape her. In the fight, Ox overpowered and strangled Griff, after which he started to come for her again, and in desperation, she had picked up Griff's revolver and shot him through the heart. Of course, she never mentioned anything about the gold or the money to anyone.

After hearing Nell's story, the sheriff went out and inspected the scene and determined that for the most part Nell's story added up. When the Strickland clan was informed of Griff's death, they stormed the undertaker, commandeered Ox's body, and dragged it through town till it fell apart. They burned his cabin to the ground. The banker informed them of Griff's withdrawal of his life savings, and while there appeared to be no way to tie the missing money to Nell, the Stricklands would forever harbor suspicions about her role in its disappearance. Privately, the family had to accept the fact that Griff was only a few brain cells smarter than the man who had killed him. There was no telling what harebrained scheme Griff had in mind when he withdrew all of his money. Yet Josh Strickland couldn't bring himself to leave it at that; he let it be known around town that Nell was a gold digger who had worn out her welcome. Nell knew it was time to leave while she still could.

Nell McGuire took the stage west to California. It took two men at the depot to lift her steamer chest onto the back of the coach and strap it into place. When she arrived in San Francisco, she deposited the gold and cash in the Wells Fargo Bank. She arranged for the money she had left in her safe deposit box in New York to be transferred to her new account. With those funds she began a new life as a rich socialite with a somewhat mysterious past, which was hardly unique in the West.

Mary O'Rourke was a street prostitute in New York. She tried to rob one of her customers as he slept, but he woke up and stopped her. She was arrested and accused of being the "Murder Madam," as the tabloids had named the infamous killer of ten fine citizens of New York. She was tried and convicted of all the killings. She went to the gallows proclaiming her innocence.

Nell changed her name to Charity Davis. Traveling in high society, she met and married a wealthy widower, Randolph Goodrich, upon whose land one of the most prestigious universities in the world would one day be built. Their marriage was blissful but short-lived. Nell McGuire alias Charity Davis became the richest woman in California after six months of marriage, when her husband died quietly in his sleep. Everyone was shocked to hear of his passing, as he had no health problems that anyone was aware of.

18

MESA VERDE

Searching for stray cattle can be a lonely and arduous task. Long, lonely days are spent on the slow trail of beasts that don't care a lick whether they get found or not, that have no idea that they are lost, and no rhyme or reason as to where they are wandering off to. Sometimes they wander off never to be found, forgotten. But in one case, cowboys doing their job made a discovery that changed southwest Colorado forever.

It was cold on the mesa that day in December of 1888, when Charles and Dickie Whiteside traversed the mesa looking for wandering strays from the Lazy 8. A frigid cold front had blown in from Canada, bringing wind gusts and blowing snow that made their search nearly impossible. Looking for a place on the flat, exposed mesa where there was shelter to start a fire, Dickie noticed a small rise where three small boulders and two straggly trees formed a small cover.

They set up a camp and got a fire blazing and coffee brewing. The snow began to abate. With visibility improving, the Whitesides could see they were actually on the rim of a large canyon. In the nonexistent visibility of the driving storm, they could easily have ridden off the edge to their deaths. Sipping his coffee, Charles surveyed the awesome vastness of their surroundings. Suddenly, he dropped his coffee as if he had been shot. Dickie dove for cover behind the rocks and pulled his Winchester from his saddle.

"Where they at, Charlie?" Dickie yelled out in panic.

"Where's who at?" Charles responded, puzzled.

"Them that shot at ya!" Dickie yelled.

Charles grimaced. "I ain't been shot, ya dumb ass. Look over there!"

The two Whiteside boys looked across the canyon, and saw something just below the rim that seemed like it was from another world. Out of a hidden and forgotten history, Cliff Palace burst into their vision. Here in the middle of nowhere was an ancient structure, the likes of which they had never seen before. Remote, untouched for centuries, here was a building bigger than any they had ever encountered, somehow built into the sheer wall of the canyon across the chasm. It encompassed over a hundred fifty separate rooms and was five stories high in places, completely uninhabited from what they could tell, like from another world. Towering walls of red adobe bricks soared up from the canyon floor. The Whitesides stood in awed silence for what seemed like eternity. Snowflakes danced in the wind and onto their mustaches under the gray winter sky.

Finally, Charles broke the silence. "It's a damned castle."

"A palace," Dickie replied. And so began the story of what would become Mesa Verde National Park.

The two Whiteside boys located a small trail that led them down into the valley below. There they found a series of dwellings that rivaled downtown Durango in size and structure. Portions were well preserved, while others were in serious disrepair. Large, broken wooden beams were scattered about. Doorways and windows looked like they were intended for people who were much smaller than the two cowboys. Pottery, utensils, and personal effects that survived the decades of harsh, unrelenting weather were strewn about. Perhaps scattered by nature, strewn about by wild animals, or some other unknown reasons, the items gave the appearance of having been thrown about by a people in a rush to leave.

"Dang, nobody's gonna believe this," Charles exclaimed, and as proof of their discovery, they filled their saddlebags with whatever recognizable items they could locate.

"I need a drink," Charles said, and they started to head back to town, lost cattle no longer a thought.

As they were gathering to depart, Dickie needed to pee. He found a small crevice in the rocks. Finished, he turned his head to the right and as he turned, he saw it. Scratched into a flat surface in the rocks was a primitive drawing, a rudimentary sketch of a person, a human being. He could not know who had made this sketch or what it meant, but it touched him with the understanding that this place had been the home of real people. He wondered, for a passing moment, where they could have gone.

News of the discovery exploded in town. Colorado is a beautiful and pristine state, with countless picturesque small towns, most of which offer the same features: natural beauty, outdoor activities, good climate. But with the cliff dwellings, Durango had within easy reach something found nowhere else in the state, something truly colossal both in physical size and historical significance, even if the latter was shrouded in mystery.

Curiosity soon led to activity, as scores of townsfolk began to trek up the mesa to visit the enigmatic ruins of a forgotten people. In the years ahead, over six hundred separate structures would be found. Thoughtful Coloradans came to understand there was no other place like it anywhere else in the West, maybe in the whole world. That uniqueness might be its salvation or its downfall, and as was true in so many things in that region back then, which of those it would become fell to the Vanderhorns and Stricklands to determine.

The discovery of the cliff dwellings was big news, not only in Durango, but also around the country, and beyond. They attracted types of people who were now interested in Durango for the first time. Tourists came to stay in the Vanderhorns' hotel and take the day tours or camping tours of the mesa, offered by local cowboys turned tourist guides overnight. Archaeologists and anthropologists from the world over came to study and learn and discover. And, as often happens in these great discoveries of history, a criminal element came to loot and pillage the artifacts, remnants of the lost people, to profit from selling to the highest bidder those items they had no right to sell.

It was a perfect fit for Josh Strickland and his henchmen.

The cliff dwellings, for all intents and purposes, lay in no-man's-land. They were so isolated that no one had bothered laying claim to the barren region in which they stood. Hell, no one had ever thought there was anything there at all besides rocks and buzzards. There was no sheriff or any other law that had jurisdiction. While most visitors showed a proper respect for the unique historical significance of Mesa Verde, for others it was a free-for-all of profiteering, theft, and, worst of all, vandalism. As the multiple sites were discovered and explored, the level of cold exploitation knew no limit. Pottery, etchings, bone tools, even mummies, were stolen and sold. The buyers were museums, universities, and rich collectors back East and in Europe, often respectable institutions that, notwithstanding their pedigree, quietly failed to inquire how the objects had come into possession of the sellers. For a time, Native American artifacts became the rage for collectors, and Mesa Verde was the motherlode source. Especially for Josh Strickland, who was making a small fortune.

Their archaeological thievery could barely keep up with the insatiable demand from buyers of all sorts. Eventually, all the major ruins were found and stripped of their valuables. As new sources of artifacts dried up, Josh Strickland perceived a new way to continue the operation. All around the valley, especially on the Rez and in the Mexican part of town, Strickland put together a network of craftsmen to create counterfeit artifacts for eager, unsuspecting buyers. A new cache of ancestral Puebloan "remains" came to market at the same time as gruesome reports of grave robbings arose from cemeteries throughout the valley. The Mesa Verde enterprise was a gold mine for Strickland. It was better than a gold mine; he didn't even need a shovel to find the "gold."

Entering his kitchen, Witt Vanderhorn could see the trouble on his wife's beautiful face. "What's wrong, Amorosa?" he asked.

"I know the cliff dwellings have been good for our business, and I am happy that so many people are coming to Durango to learn of the natives and their heritage. But I am afraid if the Stricklands aren't stopped from looting, soon there will be nothing left for anyone to see. I wouldn't be surprised if they are smuggling the adobe bricks right out of the kivas!" she lamented.

"There isn't much we can do about the looting," Witt replied. "There is no law out there, and it's too vast an area to guard. And half of Durango doesn't think there's anything wrong with taking stuff that no one has claim to, that's just been lying around for God knows how long."

"Well, we need to do something, Witt. We have to protect the site."

From the beginning of their relationship, Amorosa showed herself to be as strong as she was beautiful. When the son of the most prominent white family in Durango expressed interest in her, she thought he was either crazy or looking for easy sex with a lowly Mexican girl. She resisted his advances, but not so much as to run him off. Nor would she be intimidated into running off from him.

"Let's see if this white boy is serious," she told her mama.

Lupita Chavez cautioned, "Sincere or not, his love can't make you white, my Amorita."

Witt persisted. Slowly, Amorosa began to trust his motives and admire his character. When he asked her to marry him for the fifth time, she at last said yes, fearing there would not be a sixth. Their marriage was as great as their courtship; they were soul mates. They had suffered the scorn of loud-mouthed racists at times, but it didn't deter them from the love they shared for each other.

In their years of marriage, Witt knew how passionate and determined his wife could be. She had blazed her own trail of sorts, in becoming the first Mexican woman to properly marry a white man in Durango. When she was scorned by the ladies of the First Presbyterian Church of Durango, she won them over by virtue of her kindness and strength of character. Never forgetting her roots, she pushed Witt and the Vanderhorns to open a bilingual school for the Mexican children in the south end of town, and she always fought for the causes of justice, fairness, and equality.

An opportunity to save Mesa Verde came to Amorosa in an unexpected way. In the year 1900, Theodore Roosevelt was making a swing through the Southwest, campaigning for the vice presidency, with incumbent president William McKinley heading the ticket. As an enthusiastic naturalist and admirer of anything or anyone involved with living in the rugged outdoors, Roosevelt took a detour to survey the famous ruins on the mesa. Accompanying Roosevelt was a large entourage, including Quanah Parker, the last great Comanche chief, son of the famous captive Cynthia Ann Parker, who was rescued by Goodnight and the Texas Rangers so many years earlier. Roosevelt had befriended the chief after hearing his story and discovering their mutual interest in big-game hunting.

Sensing an opportunity, Amorosa Vanderhorn arranged a small fund-raising event for Roosevelt upon his return from the mesa, to be held at the family ranch. The Vanderhorns brought in the community leaders for a spirited show of support. After the obligatory speeches and backslapping and baby kissing, Amorosa approached Roosevelt directly, and with all the charm she could muster, she extended a hand to the future vice president and said demurely, "Mr. Roosevelt, may I have a private word with you?"

Taking his hand, she led him to a secluded area of the patio. Facing him directly and with her warmest smile, she looked into his eyes and, knowing he was fluent, she spoke to him in Spanish.

"Mr. Roosevelt, I am here to beg your help. The cliff dwellings you saw today will be gone in this generation if they are not protected. I know that you are a man of vision and have seen with your own eyes how special this place is. It needs to be saved from the criminals and smugglers and gravediggers so that it can be enjoyed for generations to come. I just know in my heart that you will be president someday. When that happens, will you do this important favor for me?"

Roosevelt smiled and kissed her politely on the cheek. Then he sat back in his chair, crossed one leg over the other, and casually lit a cigar.

As Amorosa had predicted, Teddy Roosevelt did become the twenty-sixth president of the United States, but not in the way she—or anyone else in America or across the world for that matter—could have expected. As the history books would record,

Roosevelt assumed the presidency after McKinley was assassinated by an anarchist in Buffalo, New York, in September of 1901, a little more than a year after he had visited the mesa.

Nevertheless, T.R. was reelected president in 1904, and it was during his second term, on June 29, 1906, that he signed the order dedicating Mesa Verde as a national park, forever protecting it for future generations.

Several weeks after the signing, a telegram arrived from Washington, DC, at the Durango homestead of the Vanderhorns. It said simply,

Mrs. V:

Promise kept,

TR

19

BUTCH CASSIDY

As Jim Barlow entered the Silver Dollar Saloon, he felt like he was walking into a museum. The spectacular Western-style bar was tricked out in brass and leather and glass and polished hardwoods—a sight that was a delight to anyone who appreciated brash ornamentation and fine detail. The Silver Dollar had been at the center of Durango social life for nearly a century. The original family founders, the Boltens, were still the owners, and they took great care in maintaining this piece of history. In fact, had he entered those doors at any other time over the last eighty years, he would have simply seen a slightly different version of what he was looking at today. The main room was strikingly similar to a hundred other bars in the West, with one noticeable difference. The north wall was more than three stories high and more than fifty feet wide, and the entire wall was covered with a massive blown-up version of the iconic picture of Butch Cassidy, the Sundance Kid, and the Hole in the Wall Gang.

Barlow was staring at the picture when he was interrupted by a greeting that seemed both friendly and coarse at the same time.

"I'm Sam Bolten and this is my place. Can I get you something?"

"I'll have a cup of coffee, please."

"Sure thing," Bolten answered cheerfully. "Is there something I can do to help you?"

Barlow introduced himself and carefully explained his attempts to get to the truth about his daughter's death, alluding to his concern that there was more to it than the authorities were willing to tell him. He confessed that he was getting nowhere.

"Some people have said you might be able to help me put all these pieces together, especially how the Stricklands might be involved," he hinted.

"Patty was a fine girl, just made bad choices about her men, I guess. She would come in here from time to time, now and then with that asshole Buck. I couldn't really tell if she was interested or intimidated. But beyond that, I hate to disappoint you, but I don't know much." Sam shrugged.

"I see," Barlow said. "And you don't have any notion about whether this Buck Strickland, or maybe somebody in his family, or one of his buddies, might have had something to do with my little girl's death?" He used those words deliberately, hoping to appeal to some shred of sympathy from the bartender.

"No, I'm afraid I don't, Mr. Barlow," Sam said, his face deadpan, the tone of his voice becoming stern again.

Barlow sighed at another dead end. He could tell he wasn't going to get anywhere with Sam Bolten either—or so he thought. After finishing his coffee, he said, "Thanks for your time, Sam," and he started to get up to leave. But then Sam spoke up, his voice more kindly.

"Can I tell you a story, Jim? You got a little time, maybe?" Sam asked, almost pleadingly.

Barlow looked Sam in the eyes; the old man seemed sincere. Curious, Barlow smiled and said, "Okay, go ahead." He sat back down.

Sam ordered up some drinks and food, signaling they might be there awhile.

"You see that picture up there on the wall?" Sam asked, gesturing toward the colossal mural.

"See it? How the hell could I miss it?"

Sam laughed almost uncontrollably. "Well, sir," he continued, "there's an important connection between this place and old Butch, and that connection was that the Silver Dollar was his favorite hangout in Durango. More than once the dollars that he—let's just say that he 'appropriated' in one of his adventures—that money was spent over this bar, gambling at these tables, and taking a ride with one of the girls up those stairs, sometimes sitting right there in the seat you're sitting in. Now you might think you know about Butch, maybe from that movie Hollywood made about him some years back, but there's so much more than that. They left out the best parts, probably because they didn't have the inside scoop. But I have the real story, because my grandpa tended the bar here back then and knew those guys personally.

"Hollywood got the beginning of the story right," Sam continued. "He was born Robert LeRoy Parker in the Utah territory. He spent his early years bouncing around the West, ranching, riding, butchering—that's where he got the nickname, by the way—and dabbling in petty crimes. His associates came and went with the seasons and years until he met up with the Sundance Kid. They liked and respected each other, and they seemed to give each other the confidence to go bigger in their ambitions. Their first big job was when they hit the San Miguel Bank up in Telluride. Took it for twenty-one thousand dollars, which would be the equivalent of over a quarter million today. Now, the Hollywood story said that when Butch did a job, he would immediately hightail it for the Hole in the Wall, up to Wyoming. Truth is, Butch was really smart. He was great at public relations and currying favor. He knew instinctively that he had a talent for crime, that this was just the beginning, and he wanted to make friends for the future. People who would lie for him, help him hide out, provide horses as he needed them, cover his tracks whenever he was forced to abscond, that sort of thing. So don't you know it that most of his take in that heist never left the area. He spread that money around like manure everywhere, including Durango, including this establishment. He was so likable and generous that when Durango heard Butch did a job, everyone here felt like they were about to get a payday too."

"Didn't it bother anyone that this was stolen money?" Barlow asked.

"The way they saw it, with old Butch's help, was that the rich guys back East was stealing from the West, taking our natural riches and resources but giving nothing back to the small folks who called the West home. The way Butch put it, he was just the middle man evening up the score, of course taking a cut for himself, which no one seemed to mind. Butch would come into town, throw a party for a few days, and invite everyone, including law enforcement if they were inclined to give a wink, which they usually did. At the end, he would always walk to the door, tip his hat, and say, 'There's no friends like old friends.' And he'd disappear.

"Butch and the gang did a few of their jobs here in Colorado, but they really spread it around Wyoming, Montana, Idaho, Utah. Durango was just off the outlaw trail, so we saw a lot of him. He was always on the move, and always a friend to everyone. I don't know if he was just affable or calculating, but it sure worked.

"Now, Butch and Sundance and those guys were famous for what they called the Great Train Robbery up in Wyoming. That might have been the most famous, but the sweetest I think was when they robbed the Durango and Silverton train the year before."

"I haven't heard of that one," Barlow admitted.

"Here's the way my grandfather told it to me. The train brought supplies and payroll up to Silverton and brought silver back down to be sold to the smelters. Butch figured the payroll shipment would be easy takings. So, the gang hatched a plan. They all hid up around Clarke's Bluff, right up there next to Route 550, where the grade starts to get steeper. Butch and Sundance perched themselves above to jump on the train as it went by, while the rest waited below with the horses for the getaway. They hopped on, made their way up to the engine, drew their guns on the engineer and fireman, and quickly brought the train to a stop. They raced to the money car, threw open the safe, and shoved the loot into a bunch of canvas saddlebags. Then they jumped out onto the pair of horses that Flat Nose and Harvey—guys in the gang—had brought up and positioned perfectly, and they all rode off together with ten thousand dollars or more, maybe a hundred grand today. The whole thing didn't take thirty minutes. Not a bad day's work. And do you know why it went so smooth?"

"Why?" Barlow was growing more curious.

"Because everyone was in on it." Sam laughed. "The conductor, the engineer, the ticket guy, the guard at the safe—why do you think they were able to open the safe without blowin' it up? They were all in for a share. After the deal was done, the rail's owners were told about the terrible ordeal their employees had suffered at the hands of the outlaws, and the authorities were told that the gang was last seen heading off to Wyoming. But to the contrary, everyone rendezvoused right here, at the Silver Dollar, and they had a party like no other, and a good laugh to boot. And at the end, Butch made his usual exit, got to the door, tipped his hat, and said, 'There's no friends like old friends.' And disappeared.

"When they hit that train in Wyoming, though, all hell broke loose for them. For the most part the movie got this part right. E. H. Harriman was one of the richest men in the country, and he'd had enough of getting robbed by Butch and the gang. He let loose the Pinkertons on the gang with a fury. It got so bad that they had to flee the country for South America. Everyone heard about the shootout in Bolivia and couldn't believe they were dead. Butch and Sundance were larger than life. There seems to be some controversy about what happened in Bolivia. Clearly, the federales got into a shootout and killed two gringo outlaws. But no one could ever really prove it was them. Lots of people had doubts, because it just seemed like the kind of ruse Butch would come up with to get everyone off his tail."

Old Sam finished, or so it appeared. He seemed exhausted from talking, and there was a long pause, prompting Barlow to think that was the end of the story Sam had wanted to tell.

"So, is that it? What's the point of your story, Sam?"

"Well, sir," Sam picked up again, "it's just this. Butch and Sundance, and all their cronies—they were all outlaws, can't deny it. They robbed trains, they robbed banks, and yeah, they killed a few people—mainly the people that tried to stop 'em from robbing banks and trains. But in a strange way they were tied to this community, to Durango and maybe a dozen other poor towns across the West. They were a part of those towns. They were friendly to the regular, hardworking folks in these places, people without a nickel. But they treated 'em with respect, and they tried to help folks out when they could—as I said before, spreadin' the wealth around, spending their money in the towns, the outfitting stores, the saloons, and everywhere else, and payin' a fair price for things, too.

"And you know, despite their outlaw reputation, they never killed an innocent civilian in all their years running wild. Just you look at the way they cut in all those railroad people in the Silverton train robbery. They didn't want nobody to get hurt, really."

Sam paused once more, looking Barlow in the eyes.

"What you need to understand, Jim," Sam said ominously, "is that *that* was Butch and Sundance; that's the way those guys were. The Stricklands . . ." Sam took a deep breath and shook his head heavily, looking around as if to make sure no one else was in earshot. "The Stricklands ain't like that. Butch and Sundance were the best-hearted bad guys you could ever hope for. The Stricklands are just plain evil. You understand what I'm sayin'?"

Barlow nodded, his thanks unspoken, but realizing that it was only now that the story Sam wanted to tell was complete.

"Good," Sam said. "And honestly, Jim, that's all I got to say." He seemed relieved to have said his piece.

Message received, thought Barlow. He wanted to lighten the mood once again.

"So, what do you think?" he inquired.

"Think about what?" Sam said, evidently confused.

"Well, did Butch and Sundance die in Bolivia at the hands of the federales?"

"Oh, that!" Old Sam laughed, then got serious. "I don't know what I think, but here's what I do know. My grandpa told me that 'round about 1923, twenty years after the news came out about the shootout in Bolivia, a man pulled up out front in one of the first motorcars seen in these parts. Horseless carriages, they called them. The driver got out slowly and walked in with a step that had seen better days. He stopped at the door and took a long look around. He was well dressed and had piercing blue eyes. His face looked both familiar but also different, like you could almost remember it from somewhere but not quite. Back then we didn't have the wall-sized picture up yet, but we did have the photograph that it was made from hanging on the wall behind the bar. The stranger sat at the bar opposite the picture and seemed to stare at it for the longest time.

"Grandpa observed this, as he poured the man a beer from the tap, and when he set the glass in front of him, he finally said to the man, 'Would you like a closer look at that picture?' The man only nodded solemnly, so Grandpa took it off the wall and handed it to him. The stranger held it in his hand like a long-lost treasure, the way Grandpa told it.

"Grandpa said, 'That's the Hole in the Wall Gang. They ran wild around here at the turn of the century.' He started to point and name the men in the picture, you know. 'That one there is . . .'

"But the stranger interrupted, started namin' them himself—'Harvey Logan, News Carver . . . ,' movin' his finger from face to face, 'Flat Nose Currey, Deaf Charlie Hanks . . .' right across the picture until, until he paused and swallowed hard when he got to 'the Sundance Kid.'

"'You forgot Butch,' Grandpa pointed out. But the stranger just smiled benignly. So Grandpa just continued on, saying, 'They used to come in here a lot, all of these guys. They had a lot of friends here, and lots and lots of good times. We like to think of them as part of this place.'

"The stranger said, 'You might think about doing something a little bigger to remember them. Like something on that big wall you got over there.' He placed an enormous tip on the bar in front of Grandpa. He wiped his mouth, got up, shook Grandpa's hand, and headed for the door. He opened the door halfway and turned. He took one last fond look around the room, smiled, and said, 'Because there's no friends like old friends,' and he was gone."

20

PEDRO FLORES

Pedro Flores, that is to say, the youngest Pedro Flores, despised Buck Strickland. Though their great-grandfathers had done what they called "cattle deals" together over a hundred years earlier, the younger Pedro had a deep dislike for this gringo, who was a slob in both appearance and behavior. Pedro saw Buck as a moron, a low-intelligence, uncouth racist. As a matter of family tradition, Pedro would extend hospitality to Buck from time to time, usually when Buck had gotten himself in some kind of trouble. Most of the Stricklands who visited the Flores ranch in Juarez were passingly acceptable company. But Buck was pure asshole, and a loud-mouthed braggart to boot. Maybe it was because he was just a small-time criminal in the States, while Pedro Flores led a major cartel that was built on his great-grandfather's legacy, but he found Buck's incessant bragging intolerable. Somehow Buck was foolish enough to believe that their shared history somehow made them equals.

And yet Buck equally hated Pedro Flores, or perhaps it was just a deep and abiding jealousy. The wealth and power that had accrued to the Flores family from their humble beginnings was vastly superior to whatever modest success the Stricklands had managed to achieve. Buck's family had influence in a small county in Colorado, and not all of that influence was positive. Pedro Flores and his organization, on the other hand, influenced a nation, and had managed to promulgate a thin veneer of corporate respectability. If Buck had possessed an ounce of self-awareness, he would have realized that his temporary host made him feel insecure, and he would have protected himself from overcompensating. But he didn't.

The Flores cartel was deeply involved in multimillion-dollar enterprises like smuggling drugs and humans, and providing protection to businesses and politicians on an international scale, as well as countless legitimate businesses. Their interests reached from South America to the Canadian border. Stricklands, as far as Pedro was concerned, were petty criminals harassing old ladies and scamming retirees in a small town in Colorado. He was aware and mindful of respect for long-held family loyalties, but to Pedro's way of thinking, the reality was that nothing lasts forever. Yet here Pedro was, hosting Buck at his dining room table once again.

Buck downed another shot of tequila, bit the lime, let out a huge belch, and went into full brag mode trying to impress the other men seated at the table. His odds of success were greatly diminished by his appearance: belly protruding out of his shorts and hanging over his belt, as well as the two-day-old salsa stain on his collar. Trying his best to remind them of what a bad dude he was, he told the four men around the table of his troubles with Patty Barlow—how no woman would treat him like that and how he fixed her good.

Although they were all bored by this mundane story, one of the men asked, “What did you do?”

Buck sat up proud in his chair and said, “Just like in the old days, I got up on the ridge across from her trailer on the Calstrom ranch. I waited with my hunting rifle with the scope. I waited for her to open the door to go check the horses. I knew her schedule, so I was ready. When she opened the door, I let her have it. Nailed her in the forehead from a hundred yards.”

He looked around the table, clearly expecting to have impressed them. No one looked up from their food. So Buck pressed on.

“Then I jumped on my ATV and rode over and put a pistol in her hand. That was just for appearance and to make it easy to pass this off as a suicide. We Stricklands know how to take care of each other in Durango.” Satisfied that he had impressed the group, he stuffed a tortilla chip into his mouth.

But clearly, he was making no impression on his companions. Their faces showed nothing but boredom.

Stepping it up a notch, Buck said, “But before I killed her, I poisoned her dog. Strychnine. Took three days for that pup to die. Frothing at the mouth, convulsions, seizures—the whole works. I taunted her the whole time, kept texting her, ‘How’s yer dog doin’?’ Bitches deserved it, both of them.”

Buck pushed himself back in his chair, satisfied that this evil would win them over. The other three men at the table glanced at Pedro Flores. Upon hearing this part of Buck’s story, Pedro had abruptly stopped eating. He slowly and deliberately placed his utensils down on the table on either side of his plate. Without saying a word, he pushed back from the table, took a napkin to the corners of his mouth, and left the room, never once looking at Buck. His heart raged as he walked the long adobe hallway to his private suite. Deep in thought, he climbed onto his bed, gently pulling his prized black Lab puppy up onto his lap.

His mind raced. Killing, certainly, was nothing new or foreign to him. Police, other gang members, military, even politicians all needed killing sometimes. Even killing a woman could be overlooked, although the Flores family code forbade it.

But this gringo buffoon with the big mouth and big ego had killed an innocent dog! And he had done so in the cruelest and most horrific of ways! Pedro stroked his puppy and formed a plan. He knew, more than he wished to, of the history of these two families. Their relationship had spanned almost a century, but sometimes things go too far. The Colorado partnership was an insignificant part of their business. Buck Strickland was indiscreet. He had shot his mouth off in a stupid and unnecessary way. It no longer mattered that Bart Strickland had saved the life of his great-grandfather from the ranger posse, or that his criminal empire had begun from their "cattle deals." This Buck was a loudmouth who couldn't be trusted. The Flores family had an old saying that had well served their criminal dynasty for a century: "Leave no loose ends."

Buck was a risk. But more than that, he killed an innocent dog for no reason. In Pedro Flores's code of conduct, Buck Strickland didn't deserve to live.

21

RICK LONGFEATHER

Rick Longfeather had traveled a long way from the Rez. When the Second World War broke out, he did his duty and enlisted in the army of the government that had confined his people to their reservation on the Arizona–New Mexico border. He served in the Pacific in a special communications unit called the Wind Talkers. His native language was so complex that it surpassed the codes the military had devised to confuse the Japanese. With Rick Longfeather on one end of a radio call and another of his tribe on the other, they could have a complete conversation that was intensely monitored by the enemy, who couldn't understand anything they were saying, even though the US Army made no attempt to encrypt a thing. His team had helped in the victories at Guadalcanal, Tarawa, and Iwo Jima. They were preparing for the assault on mainland Japan when news came of the atomic bombs on Hiroshima and Nagasaki and the end of the war.

Rick returned home with extra money in his pocket due to the GI Bill. With the resources to do so, and the urge to scratch a lifelong itch, and the confidence to travel off the Rez that came from having traveled halfway across the globe and fought in the war, Rick had a deep longing to visit the ancestral lands of his people. It was that longing that propelled him northward toward Colorado on Route 66 in a red flatbed '46 Ford pickup. His destination was Mesa Verde, on the southern end of the great Colorado plateau.

According to the white men's history, the builders of the Mesa Verde cliff dwellings had disappeared without leaving a trace. Arrogance, Rick mused. He was speeding through the scrubby high desert, windows down, the hot wind blowing through the cab. His people knew from where they came. Just as the white man kept a written history, his people had kept an oral history every bit as accurate and detailed. Around campfires, on walking trails, and in kivas, this history was passed down from generation to generation with all the care and veneration that such a sacred treasure both demands and deserves. To his people, the story was never lost at all. As the miles passed, he ran the story through his mind.

> *Our People lived for over seven hundred years in the land discovered by Matu, who had trusted the vision of Alo the shaman and followed Eagle to the top of the mesa. Then, one day a new eagle appeared to Catori, the new shaman. This eagle was a skin walker, or shape shifter. He turned into a human and sat on a log next to Catori under a desert night sky that dazzled with stars. The skin walker*

carried the spirit of Matu from the Great Beyond, who said, "The days of Our People here are over. Soon, a curse will come upon this place. Our People must leave at once." Then, he transformed back into an eagle and flew off to the south. Our People followed as quickly as they could pack, and within days the cliff dwellings were completely deserted. They walked month after month as nomads, farther and farther south across the unforgiving landscape until one day, Catori proclaimed, "This is the place in the vision I received from the spirit of Matu."

Our People settled in southern Arizona and New Mexico, living there for centuries side by side in an uneasy peace with the Navajo and Hopi, never forgetting their ancestors from the mesa. To honor and continue their history, they adopted the sign of the human figure that is found in the kivas and petroglyphs throughout the Southwest, and is tattooed on Rick Longfeather's right bicep.

Mesa Verde National Park was almost untouched when Rick arrived in 1950. The designation as a national park, as well as the efforts of the Durango Historical Society established by the Vanderhorn family, had stopped the smuggling and pilfering trade, although not the dealing in counterfeit artifacts that was still a profitable business for the Stricklands. Rick pulled into the gravel parking lot just after sunrise. There was no one in sight. He discovered a foot trail that led to a crack in the canyon wall, within which stood a rickety ladder descending from the top of the mesa down into Cliff Palace. As he exited the ladder and entered Cliff Palace, Rick unknowingly passed the spot where, twelve hundred years before, Matu had etched in the rock the same figure that Rick now carried on his arm, long erased by the elements.

For a long time, Rick sat on the adobe wall and inspected the structure, overwhelmed with emotion, and somehow with memories, not of his own experience, but the racial memory of his people, every bit as real as their oral history, or the written history of the whites. His spirit was filled with visions of his ancestors arriving, building, struggling, dying, and fleeing in this place, right before his eyes. His dreaming was interrupted by an eagle that circled the canyon several times before landing in a nest, far up under the ledge at the ceiling of the canyon.

Rick looked for a park ranger. Inquiring about employment, he was hired as a maintenance worker, the first Native American employee at the park. His responsibilities included making repairs, refurbishing the dilapidated cliff dwellings, cleaning latrines, and various building projects. In time, he married a woman from his pueblo, and they started a family in Cortez, at the gate to the park. His wife, Martha, was a loving and devoted partner who bore him two sons, David and Mathias. Rick and Martha raised them with a reverence for their heritage, teaching them the oral history of Our People. When the children grew to be teenagers, the family would spend part of each summer together, on a vision quest, to hear from their ancestors and to contemplate the spiritual import of their lives. Rick was confident that his sons would keep their traditions and culture alive for future generations.

Rick was doing the same at the park. At every opportunity, he spoke to the park service about his people's perspective on the stories of the park. Always respectful and humble, he thought it strange that he, a descendant of the original inhabitants of the park, needed to work so hard to get the whites to include his input. Rick slowly pulled the story of the cliff dwellings closer to the truths of his people. He constantly offered insight and correction to the narrative of the park as it was shared with growing numbers of visitors each year. He explained the symbolism and meaning behind the construction, the purpose of the kivas, his people's creation story. He was able to educate the park service that the commonly used term to describe his ancestors, "Anasazi," was actually a pejorative, replacing it with the term "Ancestral Pueblans." In countless ways he helped to make the park more true and more respectful of those it was formed to commemorate. Over the years, as the country came to terms with its handling of Native Americans, Rick's viewpoint became more valued, to such an extent that he was promoted to the position of ranger, and was authorized to lead the educational tours of the ancestral sites.

So captivating was Rick's passion for the story of his people that his son David majored in anthropology at the University of Arizona, which he attended on a full scholarship from the Vanderhorn Family Foundation. Upon graduating, he returned to Mesa Verde as chief historian of the park. Drawing on both his formal education and the cultural heritage passed down by his parents, he helped shape a compelling vision of the park that made it one of the most visited and most authentic national parks in the country. It was one of the proudest moments of Rick Longfeather's life when David was appointed the first Native American park superintendent in National Park Service history. The tears in Rick Longfeather's eyes nearly blurred his vision that brilliant spring day as he watched Vice President George H.W. Bush swear in his son to the position. Rick lifted his eyes for just a minute to view the mesa on which the ceremony was taking place. He noticed a lone eagle rise from the canyon, soar high above the stage, make a slow turn overhead, and then disappear out of view.

22

THE SCENE

Barlow had been to countless crime scenes in his career. Despite the callous, rigorously objective, and calculating persona he had adopted and honed over the years, this time would be his most difficult test, emotionally. As he pulled into the Calstrom ranch, a wave of dread swept over him. The trailer to the right just past the barn was where his precious daughter had taken her last breath.

He had gotten no cooperation from the sheriff or the district attorney in getting access to the crime scene. Authorized law enforcement only, he had been told. Fortunately, Tom Calstrom, the owner of the ranch, had called him from Los Angeles to offer his condolences and immediately consented when Barlow asked for his permission to inspect the ranch. Access to the scene was his first real break in what had been a discouraging investigation so far, informal though it was to begin with.

"Patty was so special to my wife and me," Calstrom had said. "Our hearts are broken about her, and about Timber too. Of course you can take a look. Anything we can do to help."

The Calstroms' ranch was known as the J316. Tom Calstrom, a man of faith, had worked his way through college and law school at Pepperdine University, waiting tables at a nearby Cheesecake Factory somewhere in LA. His big break came when his college roommate was drafted in the first round by the NBA's Denver Nuggets. Calstrom became his agent and business manager. Soon, he had under contract a growing clientele of young, professional-caliber athletes and a lucrative career. Combining a love for his new second home in Colorado with his desire to help others, he developed the J316 to be both a weekend getaway for his family and a one-week-a-month sanctuary for inner-city disadvantaged kids to enjoy a dude ranch experience. Patty heard about the ranch when Tom brought some of his kids on a rafting adventure with her outfit. Patty so impressed him that he offered her a job on the spot. She accepted with the condition that she finish up her season with the rafting company.

Barlow parked at the side of the lane amid a swirl of dust. He sat for a moment, gathering his resolve, and then he exited the car and approached the trailer, taking careful note of everything he saw. The trailer was across the yard from the main house, on the other side of the corral. Tentatively, he opened the door. The trailer had not been touched since the body had been removed—and the "official" investigation closed. Prematurely, in Jim Barlow's professional opinion. The place was neat, humble, and well kept, just as he expected it would be. A cowgirl hat hung on the back of a chair at the kitchen table. In the short hallway hung a picture of Patty and Lynette at a rodeo. On the night table next to her unmade bed stood two framed photos: one of Timber, the other of Patty and Jim himself, standing together under the shade of a tree at her college graduation. On the floor was the chalk outline of where his baby girl was found dead, and a deep purple stain in the carpet, already fading. Blood. For a long time he paused. Was she dead before she hit the ground? Did she know she was dying? What were her last thoughts?

Struggling to contain his emotions, he shifted his brain into the detective compartment and began to examine the scene. He needed to make a compelling case that this was a murder, not a suicide. While his gut told him Buck had killed her, he needed evidence. He opened the door and looked around outside. He noted that the trailer sat at the top of a slight incline. Anyone shooting from just outside the entrance door would be shooting uphill, and that would be a tough shot. Not likely what happened. Next, he noted that the trailer door only swung partly open. Anyone standing in that doorway would make a very narrow target. It would need to have been a straightaway shot, taken from a precise angle.

As he scanned his eyes 180 degrees around the ranch yard, he noticed that a car had pulled up and parked, the roof and police lights barely visible over the top of the fence. He had been followed. He hadn't made any friends pressing the issue of Patty's death, so he knew he needed to be careful.

Cautiously, he continued to survey the scene. Straight away, from an elevated position. That was where the shot most likely came from. He followed a line of sight straight out, across the large lawn and driveway, and beyond the corral. In between the bunkhouse and barn his sights fixed on a small ridge about a hundred yards away, with what he estimated to be a rise of about twenty feet of elevation. His heart sank as he walked up the rise to the spot he had identified. The ridge ran as far as the eye could see in both directions. Tire tracks in the soft earth indicated that someone had been riding an ATV along this ridge. Maybe related, maybe just a coincidence. Following the tracks, he came to a spot where clearly the ATV had been parked in the heavy brush, next to a small rock formation. Slowly walking around the site, deep in concentration, he suddenly realized that he was not alone. He had let his guard down and someone had the drop on him. Defenseless, he turned to see whoever was posing a threat.

He wore the uniform of the Durango sheriff's office. He was Barlow's height, lean, with jet-black hair and eyes. His name tag read, MATHIAS LONGFEATHER. For a moment, neither one spoke as they sized each other up. Barlow relaxed as he saw no menace in the deputy. Finally, after a long silence, the deputy reached into his shirt pocket and retrieved a small item. Longfeather then extended his hand.

Barlow reached out tentatively, and the deputy dropped the item into his open hand.

A brass bullet casing.

"I believe that is what you are looking for," the deputy said, expressionless. With that, he began to walk away. Over his shoulder he tossed these words, "This never happened."

23

THE DA

District Attorney Ferguson was clearly in no rush to meet with Barlow. Calls to his office went unanswered as did emails and texts. In frustration, Barlow went to his office and staked him out. For two whole days, he sat outside the DA's office on a hard oaken bench in the city hall lobby. Finally, realizing that Barlow wasn't going to give up, the DA reluctantly invited him into his office.

Ferguson's demeanor was mostly professional and direct, when it wasn't curt and dismissive. Undaunted, Barlow deliberately and in minute detail spelled out his suspicions and his hard-fact findings about what he believed to be the murder of his daughter. All the while the DA was reading and sending texts on his iPhone, displaying little interest in the information Barlow was presenting.

After hearing, but not really hearing, Barlow's case, Ferguson leaned back in his chair, yawned, and then looked at Jim pointedly.

"Detective, you are an experienced member of the law enforcement community, and for that I have tremendous respect for you," Ferguson directed, orchestrating these remarks as if the two were in court, Barlow the witness, Ferguson the cross-examining attorney. "But as a member of that community, I think you know that what you have presented here is pure conjecture. The bullet casing you found on the ridge out there, the tire tracks, that could have been anything or anybody. People go off-roading all the time out there when the owner is away, which, as you also know, is most of the time. Some of them are hunters. Maybe someone fired a shot to celebrate something or impress the girl he took out there. Who knows? It doesn't prove anything except—and please forgive me for saying this, because I do feel your pain—except that you're a broken-hearted dad grabbing at straws. The authorities here in Colorado have ruled your daughter's death a suicide and we consider the case closed. Thanks for your time."

"Can we submit the shell casing I found for a ballistics test to see if it matched the bullet that killed my daughter?" Barlow pressed.

Ferguson got up to open the door. "Mr. Barlow, I am not going to ask the people of this state to spend tax dollars investigating a case that has already been decided."

Barlow felt as though a heavy steel door had suddenly slammed shut, creating a vacuum in its wake. Dejected and heartsick, he walked out to the street, squinting into bright Durango daylight that made him feel dizzy and disoriented. He managed to make out the sign at the entrance of the Nighthorse Coffee Shop, and he went inside. Upon entering, he noticed Lynette in a flirty conversation at a back table with a quite smitten-looking cowboy. Noticing Barlow, she excused herself and came over to say hello.

"Friend?" Barlow nodded with a sly smile.

"Gus McAllister the Third. Ain't he somethin'?" she beamed. But then, remembering the seriousness of Jim's situation, she dropped her smile and continued, "How is your investigation going?"

"Not good. I just met with the DA and he just about threw me out of his office."

"Of course he did," she replied. "Bob Ferguson is married to Rebecca Strickland, Buck's sister."

24

EMMETT STRICKLAND

When Barlow finally returned to his room at the Doubletree Inn by the river, the host at the front desk handed him a small piece of paper with a message written on it.

"Call Emmett Strickland," was all it said, and a phone number was scrawled under the words.

Calling and identifying himself, Barlow was by now not surprised that the first thing Emmett Strickland said to him was, "I understand you've been asking a lot of questions around town about my family. Let's get together and talk. Maybe I can settle your mind a bit about a few things." His tone was more menacing than friendly.

They met at a park bench on the river behind an Albertsons grocery store. It was a spot where people come to watch the rafters and kayakers and tubers pass over the gentle rapids of the Animas, bending through the middle of town. Emmett's two black Labs jumped out of the bed of his pickup as it rolled to a stop. The dogs sprinted past the Dogs Must Be Leashed sign and jumped into the river, frolicking together. The sun was setting behind the San Juans to the west, lighting the red cliffs on fire as the day was drawing to a close.

Emmett Strickland was an imposing figure, well over six feet tall with a sinewy physique that looked well worked out. Cowboy tattoos covered both forearms. He wore a brown Stetson, faded Levi jeans, and a loud-patterned flannel shirt. His boots looked custom made. A Marlboro dangled from his mouth beneath his aviator sunglasses.

"I'm sorry to hear about your daughter," he started, but there was not a shred of sincerity in his voice. "I have been hearing that you've been asking a lot of questions around town about my family." He let the cigarette smoke drift into Barlow's face.

Strickland got to the point. "Just to keep this neighborly, I wanna set the record straight. Not just about Patty and Buck but about a lot of the things you been hearing, or think you been hearing. Buck didn't have nothing to do with Patty's death. He was quite fond of her. I think he was hoping to marry her. I know he mighta been a little rough with her sometimes, and I don't approve of that. But let's face it. If your daughter wanted a sissy for her guy, she would have stayed in that Green Witch Village, back in your New York, instead of moving out to cowboy country." Strickland's derision could not have been made more plain.

Barlow bristled. But he knew enough about interrogation to let Strickland keep talking. And so Emmett continued. "I know for a fact that when Patty shot herself Buck was nowhere near her. Because he was with me."

"How can you know that when the authorities don't even know for certain when she was shot?" Barlow shot back.

"Shot herself, you mean!" Strickland snarled. "Buck and me went on a hunting trip in the national forest up towards Telluride that whole time. Barlow, I'm sure you heard a lot of stories about my family. We've been here a long time. Lots of people, especially those goddamn Vanderhorns, have been lying about my family for a hundred years. But my family made this valley. Durango wouldn't be what it is today without the Strickland family. Bart Strickland, he opened the first saloon and entertainment house. He saved the cattle ranchers from those thieving New Mexico rustlers. His sons almost rescued that Romney boy who was captive with the Ute. We brought good money here by opening up Mesa Verde to tourism. Old Bart saved Otto Vanderhorn and the sheriff in that shootout with the Atkins gang. I could go on all day about the good we've done, giving people jobs and places to have fun. We have been an engine of progress in this valley." He paused to take a drag on his cigarette.

"It's easy to sit here today and judge people in the past by today's standards, but it ain't fair," Strickland went on. "Back then it was survival of the fittest. White man, Indian, Mexican, it don't matter. Everyone was just scraping by. Life was short and hard and full of misery. Hunger, cold, illness, and early death is what it was. Those were tough times and tough people. My grandpa and such did what needed to be done to survive. Maybe they crossed some lines sometimes, but who's to say what you would do if your life was on the line? Pioneers didn't come here on vacation from their apartment in Manhattan. They were at the end of their rope. Walkin' the edge between life and death every day was a better choice than staying put wherever the hell they came from. Can you imagine? I mean, hell, cannibalism wasn't even illegal in Colorado until almost the twentieth century." Strickland snickered. "You could even eat your kinfolk, if necessary. As long as you didn't murder them first, people understood! Hell, a guy named Reynolds and three of his brothers out of Kansas got caught in a blizzard on the plains heading for Colorado, and only one survived because he ate the other three. He wasn't arrested because he had their permission! That's how rough things were. Compared to eating your family, a little robbin' or trickery don't seem so bad. At the end of the day, the strong survived, and upgraded the quality of the herd into the next generations. Sounds harsh, but life was harsh."

Barlow interrupted. "It seems like you're trying to put a positive spin on what some people would say is a long line of criminal activity, don't you think?"

Strickland's face flushed red with rage. He fought back a compelling, violent urge. Killing a man who needed killing was no big thing to him, almost like like it was hot-branded into his DNA. Yet, realizing that he had the high ground and the home field advantage, he took a drag on his cigarette. It seemed to help settle his emotion at that moment. As much as a killing might settle all this, he looked at Barlow and saw a man who was playing his hand to the full but had run out of aces. The Stricklands had won again, and that was what mattered.

"Barlow," Emmett offered, "if my daughter went to your New York City and got mixed up with a boy who was in one of those mafia families, and something bad happened to her, who would be to blame?" He glared, a deathly stare.

Strickland turned and took three steps to walk away, then paused for a moment, suddenly wheeling around to face Barlow one more time. With deliberate drama, he flicked his cigarette to the pavement, crushed it heavily with the heel of his boot, and offered one last bit of counsel.

"Here's something you should keep in mind. Out here in the West we all have the freedom to choose whose lies we want to believe. I hope you enjoy your trip back to New York and that it happens real soon. That'd be my advice, if you get my meaning." And he was gone.

25

ASESINO DE PERRO

Barlow hadn't slept well. He knew that Emmett Strickland was clearly threatening him and was not trying to conceal it. He had played his hand like someone who knew he couldn't lose. Barlow was growing desperate. He did not want to leave Durango without an answer about the death of his daughter, but his pursuit was going nowhere and now there were threats.

In a pre-coffee brain fog, he made his way to the hotel dining room and chose a booth in front of a huge plate-glass window that overlooked the river. The sun had not yet come up, and the water reflected only the pale, pastel blue of the vacant predawn sky.

He ordered breakfast—and coffee—and began checking news on his phone. His brain hurt. Patty was dead. Buck had shot her. His family was covering it up. Of those facts, he was sure. He didn't have the power or connections or leverage to push the investigation any further. He was at a dead end. In his heart, he couldn't leave this business unfinished, but he appeared to be out of options. He could only resign himself to the hard fact that there was likely to be no justice in the matter of Patty's murder.

Back in New York, he had investigated plenty of murders where justice was never truly obtained, not in any tangible sense, in the courts or otherwise. But this was his daughter, and he could not hold back the feeling, on a baser level, that her murder was going to go unavenged, her killer allowed to go scot-free. The thought occurred to him that maybe he should take care of Buck himself. His heart felt like it would burst, it hurt so much. He sat for a long time gazing out the window, becoming mesmerized by the unceasing flow of the Animas, gliding by like a metaphor for time itself.

With a start, he realized that someone had slid silently into the booth across the table from him. It was Deputy Longfeather.

"Hello, Mr. Barlow," the deputy said, as he removed his hat.

"Deputy Longfeather," Jim said, collecting himself. "Pleasant surprise to see you, I hope."

"I wanted to be the one to tell you," Longfeather responded, "before the news gets out."

"Oh? What news?"

The gravity of what Longfeather was about to tell him showed in his eyes. And a smirk that hinted of satisfaction.

"I thought you should know," the deputy began, "three days ago, the border patrol found a body hanging from a length of barbed wire slung from an old fence near the Rio Grande. The body was identified as Buck Strickland."

Stunned, Barlow reeled back into the leather seat as if someone had thrown a punch at him. He dropped his fork onto his plate, where it landed with a loud *clang*. He was suddenly aware of his heart racing furiously.

"What happened?" he asked.

"Looks like he pissed off somebody pretty good," the deputy answered without expression. "And for the last time, too, I guess. When they first found him, it looked like he had been tortured some and a gun was put in his mouth and fired. Obviously, being a murder, the coroner did an autopsy to determine the cause of death. Turns out all that nasty stuff was done to him *after* he died."

"I don't understand," Barlow said. "So what killed him?"

"It was strychnine poisoning." Longfeather hardly concealed his smile. "Musta been pretty awful."

With that, the deputy gathered his hat and began to slide out of the booth, pausing briefly, and turning to look once more at Barlow.

"Oh, and one more thing. He had a sign hanging around his neck with a message written on it in Spanish," the deputy offered.

"What did it say?" Jim asked.

"*Asesino de perro*," the deputy responded. "It means 'dog killer.'"

26

FAREWELL

Jim Barlow figured that he'd accomplished about as much as he was going to, so he decided to head back to New York. He made plans to meet up with Lynette Bouchard to thank her for her friendship to Patty and for her help in navigating the ins and outs of the powers that be in Durango. Entering the Outlaw, he noticed Lynette waiting for him in a booth by the window, so he walked over and slid into the seat opposite her.

"I heard about what happened to Buck," she said. "Everybody's talking about it. That's karma Western-style, if you ask me. Truth is, I would have shot that bastard myself if I had the chance. With Buck dead, are you satisfied that Patty's murder has been solved?"

Barlow shrugged. "I guess I am going to have to be. Not like I have a lot of options. I talked with Emmett Strickland and he made it pretty clear that I was overstaying my welcome. I am not one to turn tail and run. But seeing how the authorities handled

Patty's death doesn't give me the idea I'd get a lot of help if I take on the Stricklands. Tell me, how is it that a family with such a sketchy past has gained so much power in this town?"

Lynette paused to organize her words. "It's unfortunate that your circumstances have caused you to get the wrong view of our town. Sure, there are bad things going on here now and then, but a lot of good things, too. When you look at this community, you just got introduced in a bad way and to the wrong people. There's good people here, too. Like Gus McAllister, over there waiting for me."

She motioned with her hand in the direction of the parking lot, where a handsome cowboy waited for her, leaning against the hood of a late-model Ford pickup and looking for all the world like a latter-day James Dean in a white cowboy hat and aviator glasses highlighting his good looks. "He's a Vanderhorn on one side of the family tree. Sweet, kind and . . . handsome! He's got a heart of gold, but he comes from good stock of men and women who have kicked ass as needed around here for a hundred years, and he's more than able to do the same if the need arises."

"But it seems like the Stricklands have won, so to speak," Barlow observed.

"Maybe to you, maybe at this point in time." Lynette breathed deeply and went philosophical. "Over the years, the Stricklands learned how to use raw power, intimidation, money, and fear to get their way. But they also learned more subtle ways like family connections, marriage, and elections to gain an air of legitimacy. Let's be real. At any point in time, half the people anywhere would have questionable scruples and think maybe the Stricklands are the good guys! Many of their positions of influence actually came from elections where they won fair and square. That's the flaw of democracy. Sometimes the majority of voters can elect people who should never be allowed to run anything. That DA Ferguson is a boot-lickin' lap dog who spends his entire life kissing Emmett Strickland's ass.

"If there's one thing you learn in the West, it's that good and bad ebbs and flows over time. Sometimes the good guys seem to be coming out ahead and sometimes the bad. Over the long arc of history, it seems to swing like a pendulum. When things are good, people get complacent and bad gets a foothold. When things get too bad, folks get fed up, and demand law and order. And let's be real, everyone in the West isn't looking for a Sunday school class. To the average person, for the most part, vice is more attractive than virtue, and it pays better." She chuckled.

"Mr. Barlow, I love the Vanderhorn clan and believe they represent the best of Colorado, past, present, and future. But for every fan they have for cleaning up the place and keeping it civilized, where decent people would want to live, there's a guy who thinks just like the Stricklands, and think the Vanderhorns are useless do-gooders who are just in the way. But don't worry too much. There is a lot of good here, too. Maybe you can come back sometime, when your head is more clear, and see for yourself. The Vanderhorns and McAllisters have done so much to make this a great place to live. They still own the newspaper that old Peter started a hundred years ago. The college has a record number of students enrolled, and a large number are off the Rez on scholarships that Amorosa Vanderhorn established. Mesa Verde is a World Heritage site and tens of thousands of folks come from around the world to visit every year. Next time you're here, I'll take you out to the Vanderhorn ranch. They turned a portion into a replica of an Old West town. Witt Vanderhorn found an abandoned ghost town that had been used as a movie set. He bought it, had it moved piece by piece to his ranch, and reassembled and restored it just so folks could have an authentic Old West experience. Every night, hundreds of tourists go out there for a chuckwagon supper, good cowboy music, and authentic reenactments of events in our history, like the Atkins gang shootout. The train up to Silverton is as beautiful a ride as any in the world, and the sky at twilight will take your breath away. My only regret is that this whole Strickland business gave you the wrong impression. Like any town or city, Durango is in a constant tug-of-war between vice and virtue, and the winner ain't been decided. Maybe that's exactly how it should be."

Barlow smiled a paternal smile. "I understand," he said. "And I think you're absolutely right."

"Well, I gotta go," she replied.

Lynette stood up and signaled that she was on her way out to Gus, who was waiting patiently. She adjusted her jeans, hat, and vest, unbuttoned the top button of her blouse, looked at Jim, and said, "I got my own tug-of-war about vice and virtue goin' on these days and I'm afraid I got a really good idea whose gonna win!" She chuckled, kissed Barlow on the cheek, and as she hurried for the door, she called back, "Have a good flight home."

27

MOUNTAIN WINDS

As the Delta 767 backed away from the gate and began to taxi, Barlow looked out the window and saw prairie dogs scatter. At the La Plata airport that serves the Animas Valley, he mused, they are not just the welcoming committee but the farewell one also. Somehow it was a comforting thought, like an age-old ritual that one could rely on time after time after time. He stared at the terrain, mentally bidding his last goodbyes to the valley where he laid his only daughter to rest, knowing he likely had visited the West for the last time.

Before heading for the airport, he had driven up to Molas Pass. He had stood silently for a long time in the parking lot, gazing at the peaks that surrounded and towered over him. He had never felt so small and insignificant. He would be here on the earth alone without the daughter he loved, for just a few short years, and then he would be gone. But these mountains would be forever. Waiting until the parking lot was empty, the tourists having gone back to the lights and gaiety of the hotels and restaurants, Barlow went to his rental car and took out a simple wooden box. Patty had never expressed to him her final wishes. It never seemed necessary. Parents don't expect to bury their kids. Knowing these mountains were the place she loved most, he thought it most fitting to leave her here. He could never think of her left in some hole in the ground somewhere. That wasn't his Patty. Opening the box, he began to scatter her ashes to the wind. Although not a religious man, he said what to him was a prayer, asking God to take care of his little girl as the winds scattered forever her mortal remains, as well as all the dreams for her that he held in a father's heart.

A beam of sunlight broke through the darkening clouds and illuminated the valley as the gray ash cloud dispersed in every direction. The mountain winds spread the dust of a life cut short to the firs and the aspens, to the mountain flowers, and even to the snow-covered peaks above. He hoped that her ashes would help make this soil fertile for the dreams of others who would come to this rugged and beautiful land, and that those who followed would live to see those dreams fulfilled. He would never know that some of the ashes carried in the wind currents down the valley and would come to rest on the graves of Charlotte Vanderhorn and her daughter Victoria, whose lives, like Patty's, had ended too young.

He hadn't exactly solved his daughter's murder, but he knew what had happened. Justice had somehow been done in a very Western way. In the process of investigating Patty's story, he had learned the story not only of Durango, but also of the larger Old West, how the stories, facts, and legends all blurred and ran together, indistinguishable from one another. The truth about the Old West was based largely on who was telling the story. Winners, losers, good and evil, heroes and villains, all floated interchangeably across the pages of history. The story of the Vanderhorns and Stricklands was a story about how the forces of good and evil shaped the West, and, with other names and locations, continues to shape the West to this day. He learned that history in the West doesn't go in straight lines, but weaves like a rainfall flowing about as it finds its turbulent way down a canyon. Many of the legends and myths of the Old West were in fact based on accidents and misunderstandings.

He tried, but couldn't find the words to sum up his time in the Valley of Lost Souls. Just like he couldn't find the words to express the fiery hues that reflected off the desert as the sun slowly faded in the west when his plane taxied to take off. He thought about all those who had been part of the making of this part of Colorado, of the cliff dwellers and Chief Ouray, the settlers and the prospectors, the railroad men and the ranchers, the gunfighters and train robbers. So many characters, so many stories. He thought about all those who gave up everything to move to this beautiful and challenging place—this often unforgiving place. Those people were true pioneers, to come out here to make a life for themselves out of grit and determination and hope. Characters with both good intent and bad came to the West with hopes and dreams and ambitions as big and wide open as the land they came to inhabit, sometimes winning, sometimes not, sometimes giving their lives for the simple pleasure of being part of the unique story of cowboys and miners, of chiefs and sheriffs, of good guys and bad, and all the rest that together wrote the history of the West. He mused, that was what his Patty had done. In her own way, she was part of the great sweeping panorama that is the American West.

He thought of the only thing Emmett Strickland said to him that was worth remembering: "Out here in the West we all have the freedom to choose whose lies we want to believe."

In that thought, he found peace. He tilted his seat, closed his eyes, and drifted off to sleep.

AFTERWORD

This book is intended to be a love letter to the Old West, and Durango, Colorado, in particular. I was born in 1957 and grew up on a nightly diet of *Bonanza*, *Gunsmoke*, *The Rifleman*, and all those. All three major networks featured Westerns in their nightly offerings. Our family made an annual pilgrimage to the local drive-in for that year's John Wayne movie. He was the number one box office draw each year for most of my childhood.

My first movie date was to see *Butch Cassidy and the Sundance Kid* starring Paul Newman and Robert Redford. Little did I know I would have the opportunity to ride those same lands and jump off that same cliff just a few short years later.

I am not sure at what age I realized what I was watching was fiction. Like in this book, it's kind of a blur. My fascination with the West and the cowboy life took a hiatus for a few decades. Then, in the early 1980s, I saw a travel clip on TV about the Durango and Silverton Railroad and, on a lark, flew out with some friends one

Memorial Day weekend to visit the West—the real West—for the first time. A high school friend who was living in Durango hosted us. She had visited Durango for a summer job after college and never came home. So in her own way, she is part of this story.

Having grown up on the East Coast and spending time surfing the world, I couldn't imagine intentionally going somewhere with no ocean. Seeing Durango for the first time and the surrounding 14K peaks, I had the feeling of going home, even though I'd never even been there before. John Denver had been right. I fell in love with the West at first sight.

It was so different back then. I remember pulling into Mesa Verde National Park to visit the cliff dwellings on Memorial Day weekend. We parked in an empty parking lot. Literally. There were no other cars. We waited about twenty minutes for a ranger to drive up and point us to a ladder down into Cliff Palace. We checked the ruins out, unaccompanied. Today you need advance tickets for a guided tour. Things change.

I have visited Durango several times over the years, each time bringing new family members with me—my wife, my children, and my in-laws—to share the experience. Durango opened our interest in the West and we have also adventured to other parts of Colorado, as well as Wyoming, Montana, Arizona, and Texas. It is notable to me that to an extent, Durango remains relatively unknown to travelers I speak to. Most have stories to share about Yellowstone, the Grand Tetons, and other well-known and very popular places in the West, but rarely Durango.

I have never had a disappointing trip to the West. Every destination has its unique appeal. For me, the special draw of Durango is manifold. It is just big enough. It has a cowboy appeal. It is a great home base from which you can visit ancient desert canyons one day, high elevations the next, do water sports on lakes and rivers the next, followed up by a visit to a World Heritage site in the national park. I'd like to note, here, that the national park is great, but for my family and me, the real experience of the cliff dwellings was most appreciated when we visited the ruins in the Ute Mountain Tribal Park, which I believe is a must way to get the true history of the area from a Native American perspective.

To my thinking, Durango is the perfect setting for a tribute to the West, to its legends and lies and realities. It is also a great place to visit. I hope this book has given you a sense of this special place.

ABOUT THE AUTHOR

DOUG TWOHILL has held a lifelong love of the Old West, which inspired *A Death in Durango*, his first book. He has been married to his wife, Cindy, since 1987. Along with their six adult children, they live in South Florida and visit the West regularly.